A Sword Unsheathed

Helen Godfrey Pyke

Nampa, Idaho | Oshawa, Ontario, Canada
www.pacificpress.com

Cover design by Gerald Lee Monks
Cover illustration by Marcus Mashburn
Originally published in 1970.

The author assumes full responsibility for the accuracy of all facts and quotations as cited in this book.

Heritage Project
This book is part of the Pacific Press® Heritage Project, a plan to republish classic books from our historical archives and to make valuable books available once more. The content of this book is presented as it was originally published and should be read with its original publication date in mind.
You can obtain additional copies of this book by calling toll-free 1-800-765-6955 or by visiting www.adventistbookcenter.com. You can purchase this as an e-book by visiting www.adventist-ebooks.com.

ISBN 13: 978-0-8163-3520-6
ISBN 10: 0-8163-3520-6

13 14 15 16 17 • 5 4 3 2 1

Contents

Glossary

Bernicia—northern province of Northumbria (R. H. Hodgkin, *History of the Anglo-Saxons,* p. 275.)

Bower—low log building where women and small children had their chambers

Byrnie—iron mail tunic (Marjorie and C. H. B. Quennell, *Everyday Life in Angh-Saxon, Viking, and Norman Times,* pp. 11, 12.)

Coracle—a short boat made of wicker frame stretched with skins—used by Scots (Irish of this tribe during seventh century)

Eorl—word from which modern word earl is derived—a war leader of great importance who had been given lands under the conquering Anglo-Saxon princes

Northumbria—northeastern kingdom in England—in A.D. 632 from the River Tweed to the Humber

Picts—barbarian tribe living in what is now Scotland

The Mark—a boundary line where visitors must stop and announce themselves before approaching a ton (Quennell, p. 10.)

Ton—enclosed agricultural settlement surrounded by a wooden stockade with a narrow door (Hodgkin, p. 218.)

Wergild—the price exacted as a fine for killing someone in Anglo-Saxon England—1,500 shillings, the price of a cow being one shilling, was the fine for killing a prince (Winston S. Churchill, *Birth of Britain,* p. 66.)

Woden—war god of the Anglo-Saxons

Introduction

If you come upon a page of Anglo-Saxon manuscript writing in a history book, you will have trouble reading it. Yet such writing is the ancestor of all modern books printed in English. And if you walked into an English settlement of 1,300 years ago, you would understand no more of the conversation than if you were visiting the most remote valley in New Guinea.

The people would look strange to you in their rough clothing. The homes would seem dirty and cold, even those belonging to men and women of noble birth or the ruling families of the many tiny kingdoms that made up the British Isles in those days.

Still, many things would make you feel at home in the England of 1,300 years ago. A Saxon's ideas of personal liberty and the importance of law, his hospitality and sense of honor, his loyalty to his family, have been preserved through the centuries wherever men speak the English language.

The Saxons were valley dwellers, building their settlements along the rivers, plowing the heavy soils the earlier inhabitants of Britain had left untouched. They gathered around a war leader, an eorl, and built his ton, or settlement, surrounding it with log walls for protection from enemies or wild beasts.

In their hearts lurked fear of the hundred or more gods they worshiped. But most of the Saxons of A.D. 630 wished they could rid themselves of the old superstitions.

I want to tell you how this happened to many tons in northern

England along the English Channel. If you are descended from the Anglo-Saxons, your ancestors have not always been Christians. Someone came as a missionary to them, even as in the past three hundred years missionaries have spread the gospel from Europe to the Americas and Africa and Australia and the islands around the world.

Picture yourself in northern England in A.D. 633. Imagine a strongly fortified but primitive settlement surrounded by farms and dense oak forests. Then see if you have anything in common with a boy of that time and place—a boy eager for manhood, but not quite sure he is ready for such important choices as he must make, not quite sure he is ready to carry a Saxon sword and pull it from its sheath.

Chapter One

LUTHWIN KICKED old Thundor the ox, hurrying him up the slope toward the ton. But, tired from plowing the heavy clay soil, the animal's fastest trot was too slow. The youth tried to hide his embarrassment as he passed the gateman. He jumped from Thundor's back, caught his balance, and ran for the great hall.

At the door he halted, peering inside at the circling clouds of smoke rising around the log fire. Then he went straight to Hunwold.

"Father!" he panted. "Someone is coming along the river. And they did not sound their horn at the Mark."

His father frowned. Luthwin knew he feared invasion might come even late in the season from the Picts or the Scots.

"In these troubled times you are wise to warn me," Hunwold said. "Did you see only one man or many approaching, Luthwin?"

His son bit his lip. "I saw many horses, Father," he faltered. "Ten, maybe, and all of them with riders. They were beautiful horses, Father." He felt his face redden when Hunwold smiled indulgently. Why did his father always treat him like a child? After all, he was twelve years old.

"Always you see horses and not men! The horses are not armed. Did you see if the men carried weapons?" Hunwold asked.

Luthwin shook his head. Why had he not noticed? "But they were dressed in red, some of them. And one man wore a gold clasp on his cloak."

"Ah, so they are important," his father mused. He rose from his high oak chair.

Luthwin waited to let the thanes follow his father to the door. He heard the clatter of the swords and spears they picked up outside.

It would look silly, Luthwin decided, to ride the old ox behind his father's men as they set off toward the river. He climbed up high into a spreading oak just outside the log ramparts that enclosed the ton. From there he could see his father moving rapidly down the road to the River Tweed.

"Ho, Luthwin! Why are you perched like a raven up there?"

Startled, Luthwin glanced down at his Celtic slave standing at the bottom of the tree.

"They did not blow their horn," he said. "And if you had brought my horse in as I ordered, I would not be perched up here. I would be riding with proper dignity on Twi with my father and his men."

He swung around the bough where he had sat and slid down the trunk. "Wallen, I had to ride that plodding old Thundor all the way from the river plowing to tell Hunwold!"

Wallen grinned, and Luthwin knew that the slave did not let the scolding upset him. "Thundor is not a dignified mount," he agreed. "But I have your horse now. He broke out of his pasture again."

The two boys rounded the barricade and went through the narrow gate.

"Do we have visitors?" Wallen asked.

Luthwin sniffed. "They might find themselves thrust through with a Saxon sword if they come up on us like thieves without warning," he said. Noticing that Ceda had a roast turning on the spit in the wattle cookshed, he could not resist the urge to rub his stomach.

Wallen pulled at his sleeve, nodding knowingly. "Mother," he called, "do you have any sweets for the young master? He will soon starve."

The slave cook waved to them.

Luthwin watched her spread honey on oat cakes for him. Laughing, he licked the honey that dripped from the edges when he ate the first cake. "Ceda, you are worth half my father's estates," he commented.

The Celtic woman clasped her hands over her ruddy elbows, chuckling. "And you, lad, are worth ten sons to your father."

Luthwin noticed she looked at her own son with pride. He shared her pride in Wallen, admired his tough muscles and dark eyes, merry with laughter. But Wallen was a slave, Luthwin reminded himself. A shout made him turn around.

His brother sat in the watchtower, and now he pointed down the road. "Lord Hunwold returns with some unlikely guests!"

Luthwin looked out the gate at the troop moving ahead of Hunwold's men. "Who are they?" he shouted to Raedfrith. "Do you know them?"

"Not at all!" his brother returned loudly. "But one wears a tunic flowing to his feet like a woman's, and it is all white. It has a hood, too. He wears a crimson cloak and scarf with gold decorations." Raedfrith took one more look, then started down the ladder, his red hair tumbling over his eyes.

Standing just inside the gate, Luthwin watched the men come into the enclosure. His father took the lead, with six armed thanes riding behind, ready to act if the visitors should make a hostile move.

The Saxon youth counted eleven strangers—ten richly dressed, and one servant leading the first horse. Its rider was the most important of the group, Luthwin decided. Around his half-shaven head hung a hood of white wool, and the flowing length of his tunic did indeed reach to his stirrups, where his feet, encased in blue slippers, gripped the sides of his mount.

He is nervous riding, Luthwin thought. But why should a man so richly dressed be uneasy on a fine horse? Surely he rides everywhere he goes. His shoes are not meant for walking.

In front of the great hall they dismounted. Eldred, his father's most trusted thane, stood at the door to take the spears from the nine visitors who carried them.

Ceda called to Wallen. "There will be feasting tonight," she said. "Come now and help me prepare."

Her son hurried after her, and Luthwin walked to the hall. "Who are they?" he asked Eldred, sitting down on the bench beside the door.

"They claim they are from King Edwin," the old thane said, his face betraying skepticism. "But they seem to come to dazzle our eyes and make us think we know nothing. They speak of teaching us new ways and new gods. And already we have more gods than any people can use. We become impoverished with sacrifices!" He shook his gray head. "Well, we will listen with true courtesy."

"And have your mead," Luthwin added, winking.

"And have our mead," Eldred muttered. He leaned the spears of the visitors against the wall and went inside.

It was dark before Hunwold called for the food. Luthwin went into the hall with Raedfrith before the women came with the roast meat and bread and drink. They sat on the bench out of the way of the older men and listened with respect. In his seat high on its platform at the center of the hall, Hunwold listened, too. The most important stranger sat opposite him. His dark, proud face was strangely thin, his eyes bright and piercing.

"Your king, the noble Edwin, has been a Christian for years, as you know," the man said. "And it has been his wish that all his people should embrace the faith of the true God and His Son, Jesus Christ. For this reason, your king has sent me to you to teach you this religion."

"We have worshiped the gods of our fathers until now," Hunwold interrupted. He laid his hands on his knees as if he intended to get up from his chair. But he settled against its carved back instead. "It is our custom to pay tribute to Thor and Woden. I myself am descended from Woden."

The man in the white tunic seemed to pay no attention. "We are men learned in the schools of the countries to the south—from Rome." He smoothed the golden chain that hung from his middle. "We have instructions to teach you more enlightened ways. If you will listen to the wisdom we bring, you will prosper under the blessing of Heaven. Have patience, though, and hear us, for I am Paulinus, a bishop of the true and holy church."

"Do you see his fine purse?" Raedfrith whispered.

Luthwin nodded. "It hangs like a plump sack of curd cheese ready for the table. I suppose it is full of coins."

The women brought food then, and in spite of the guests, who sat aloof on their side of the hall, loud talk and louder laughter rang through the wooden building as the men ate.

Luthwin took his knife from his belt and cut meat from the joint and a large chunk of bread. He drank from Raedfrith's mead until he felt dizzy. His ears rang with voices that hummed and roared. Sleep overpowered him, and he did not wake up until dawn. With the fire gone down to ashes, the hall was cold.

Stumbling across the prone bodies of thanes sleeping on the straw on the floor, he went outside, gulped deep breaths of air, and walked toward the stables. Already the women went about their chores—milking, feeding the cattle, washing the linen. Ceda fanned a smoking fire in the cookshed.

"Can you feed me something?" Luthwin asked, warming his hands over the slow flames. She brought him warm milk and bread.

"What is the business of these visitors?" she asked. "They are strange men indeed. They would not sleep in the guest chambers, but asked for finer rooms, and your mother had to let them have her own bower."

"They speak of a new religion." Luthwin swallowed a mouthful of bread. "They say we ought to learn the faith of Christ, which is the religion of Edwin."

Ceda shook her head. "That is nothing new. My people have known that story since the days of the Romans. I heard it myself from my grandmother when I was a child. But that was before the Saxons moved as far as this valley," she added. "My people were free in those days—and proud and independent."

"What is it all about?" Luthwin asked. "I could not understand all they said, for they did not speak our tongue well."

She shook her head again. "Your people brought with them the worship of Woden, and say he is your ancestor. Maybe he is."

"He must be given devotion to protect our lands and crops and our men of war," Luthwin explained. He watched her bring an iron pot and set it on the stone hearth.

"Christians worship a God who made everything and lives still in a heaven place," the slave woman continued. "He is not at all like Woden. He is not always angry and ready to punish with pestilence and war."

Luthwin considered what she said while he finished his milk. Although he wanted to ask Ceda more, he did not want her to think he was really interested in the new faith. He must not commit himself to anything Hunwold had not heard completely and decided for the whole settlement.

"Really, I do not know much about this Christian God," Ceda remarked, her back to him. "But it does seem wiser to worship One who made everything. He must be a God of greater power than any of the many gods the Saxons worship."

The Saxon youth thought of the gaiety of the spring festivals his family celebrated, and of the times when everyone came in processions behind Sigbert the priest to a table spread with dainties under the oak trees.

"Does this religion have feasts?" He broke one last chunk of bread for himself.

"I do not remember feasts." Ceda chuckled. "But then, I never was so foolish about food, either."

"I would miss the feasts of the Earth Mother, and the feasts when we go to war," Luthwin said to himself as he walked across the courtyard.

During the day he stayed around the enclosure. In the great hall Hunwold talked seriously with the bishop and his men. Wallen worked in the field, driving the oxen before the plow. Raedfrith watched the smith forge his new suit of ring mail. Luthwin grew tired of hearing him brag that he would wear it to battle next spring.

When the sun passed the peak of the Woden temple, Luthwin slipped unnoticed into the hall and sat in the shadows. Talk went on endlessly, and his father was growing impatient.

"You may be a bishop, as you say, of the great Christian Father in Rome," Hunwold exploded at last; "but I have never been there, and he has never been here. He is neither of our kinsmen nor our race!"

"Yet he rules men of all races," the bishop countered.

"Ah!" The Saxon leader smiled. "He is not likely to come so far to do battle, or even in friendship. And even Edwin rules his kingdom from far regions that have not always been a part of this nation."

"He is your king," the visitor persisted.

Hunwold stood up, his face glowing his pride. "I must choose for myself and for my own people, for we live on the very rim of Edwin's kingdom, bearing the Pictish burden almost alone. We do this for Edwin, but without his aid."

The white-robed bishop firmed his mouth into a knowing smile. "You have had no trouble with the Picts for three years."

"Only because I have inspired them with dread for my strength," Hunwold said. "I am known as far as Strathclyde, and Edwin himself pays attention to me." He straightened his shoulders. "Am I not the son of a royal line through my father, who was the younger son of a prince? I tell you, we are descended from the great Woden himself, and other warriors, both noble and famed." He thumped his spear handle on the floor. "We owe allegiance to no man unless we choose!"

"Aye!" The murmur echoed from bench to bench where the warriors listened.

"You are a worthy leader, an honor to your forebears, Hunwold," Eldred said with feeling. "There is not a one of us who is not proud to follow you in battle or in peace. You are an eorl both generous and noble."

The bishop coughed and clapped his hands. "Edwin did not send me to listen to your boastings!"

Everyone turned to look at him. He trembled with rage.

"Edwin sent me to be your teacher. And he commands you to pay attention to my words. For he knows they are words to bring you life hereafter."

Hunwold raised his hand to silence the assembly. "Then speak," he muttered, sitting down.

"You have known only death and the hard things of life," the bishop said, his voice suddenly soft and eloquent. His hands still moved nervously over the chain in his lap. "We bring you news of life after a man dies. He who submits to baptism and the holy cleansing as Edwin has instructed will be assured of riches and bliss everlasting. But he who refuses to take this rite will doom himself to the torments of a fire that burns forever. Thus he shall pay the penalty for his wickedness."

Luthwin shuddered. Ceda had talked about the heaven place, but she did not mention fire. He looked at the flaming hearth in the center of the room and recalled the time he fell into it as a child. He still remembered the pain in his hands when he thought of it. He had lain there only a moment until his father pulled him out. What would it be to have his whole body aflame for years? forever? He wished he had not heard about it. It was much easier to believe in the reward of warriors the way his family had always taught.

But the bishop spoke with pleasure, he thought, of the terrible punishment. "If you wish to be safe from hell, you must submit," he said, his face glowing with a sense of power.

"What then is this baptism?" Hunwold leaned forward intently. "Is it the magic of your religion that can protect us against so fierce an enemy as death?"

The bishop smiled. "Certainly it can."

"Speak on," the Saxon eorl said.

"It is but a simple matter. I could baptize your whole people in the river we followed. And if you promise allegiance to our lord the pope, and do faithfully obey all his commands, you need have no fears, for we have the keys to the home of the blessed, which shall be theirs as soon as they die."

"Ah!" Luthwin whispered. So *that* was what he had in his bulging purse! Certainly he had many keys to fill it so full and make it so heavy.

Hunwold shook his head. "It is not our custom to swear allegiance to strangers," he objected. "We must think the matter over for a time before we give our word."

He stood and waved for the company of men to go with him, leaving Luthwin alone in the great hall—alone with the smell of wood and smoke and leather hangings. He let his eyes roam over each familiar timber of the roof and all the intricate designs on the shields hanging from the lowest beam.

The religion of Christ, he thought, asked a great deal. To a God who made the world he might promise obedience. But he did not want to give his freedom to some bishop to do always what he said. A Saxon was a free man. His father had told him that a thousand times. No man ruled a Saxon against his will.

Luthwin jumped up, trying to forget all that he had heard. He would find Raedfrith. But would his father decide to become a Christian? The question nagged in the youth's mind. Would Hunwold pledge all his family to obey the bishop and his lord the pope? Would they all become the pope's men now?

"Do not be foolish," Raedfrith scoffed when his brother told him his fears. "Saxons give a lot of show to their worship, but Sigbert is the only grown-up in the ton who really believes all the nonsense about gods with real power. And he has good reason to believe. He gets a lot of gold and finery for his priestly services." Raedfrith laughed.

"Hunwold, our father," he continued, "is too wise to change his ways quickly. He will fight for Edwin because he has given his word, but I doubt he will follow the king in this matter. Father likes the old ways best. They are more comfortable."

Luthwin examined Raedfrith's mail tunic, running his fingers over the bright iron rings. "You have a fine suit of armor," he said. "When

I am sixteen years old, I, too, will dress myself for fighting. But now I can at least practice. I will go after my sword."

For a whole month, since he had his twelfth birthday and received his sword and horse, Luthwin had practiced with Raedfrith on the slope beyond the ton. He knew his brother was still careful not to strike him too hard, for until recently Luthwin had only a wooden sword. He and Wallen used to play together, using similar ones.

"Now you are too old to play with a slave," Raedfrith had told him on his birthday.

In the log building stretching along the high side of the enclosure, Luthwin went to his own chamber. In the oaken chest he found his prize, took it carefully from its scabbard, and carried it out into the sunlight.

"You took long enough," Raedfrith chided him. "I cannot play with you the whole afternoon."

Luthwin flashed the sword, admiring the way it handled. "I do not plan to spend the time playing," he said. "I want to have you show me just how to thrust and strike and swing the way you will do in battle."

Raedfrith laughed with pleasure. "Then we will not play today. We will practice warfare."

The sword weighed more than Luthwin thought. In a little while both his arms ached from swinging it. But Raedfrith had not tired, although his weapon was much bigger.

The younger boy wiped his face on the sleeve of his tunic again and again until it was wet, as wet as the back of his shirt, where a stream of sweat ran down his spine. He shivered in the wind that swept up the hillside from the meadows along the river. Clouds covered the sun now, and soon a shower would wet the land.

Raedfrith also noticed the clouds. "I do not mean to get soaked," he said finally. "Come, Luthwin. You have had enough for today. And so have I." He pushed his reddish hair away from his face. "Another day I will teach you more."

The cooking shed felt warm. They sat before the fire and nibbled dry wheat cakes, watching Ceda stir a pot of broth. Across the enclosure they could hear voices rising in the great hall. Luthwin looked at his brother. Raedfrith raised his eyebrows and cocked his head to listen.

Eldred came out of the great hall, stationed himself beside the spears at the door, and kept looking inside.

A shout rang across the courtyard. "We will not be subject to this man!"

Other voices repeated the words. And the bishop's servant rushed out to the stables. In a moment he returned, leading his master's horse.

His long nose pointing straight ahead, the bishop walked past Eldred to his animal. His servant helped him as he struggled to mount while trying to remain dignified. The bishop looked at the threatening sky, pulled his hood over his head, and fastened his cloak more securely with its golden clasp while he waited for his men to get their horses.

"I shall tell your noble King Edwin of this rebellion!" he shouted, his voice breaking on a high pitch. "You have flouted his commands and the commands of the Church. You have committed all the innocent youths of your household to the fires of damnation forever. Indeed, your king shall hear of this matter. And he will not take lightly your decision."

"You may tell Edwin," Hunwold thundered from the doorway of the hall, "that I will come to him myself to talk of this business. You may tell him that he will see me face to face, for I will not have your lying tongue bearing him false tales." He raised his spear and shook it in the air. "Now you and all your company be out of my lands. It is not our custom to attack guests within our gates."

The bishop gripped his reins and trembled in his saddle. The horses trotted out through the gate, and Luthwin wondered if the churchman would manage to stay mounted all the way back to Edwin's court.

"They are gone, and we are not baptized," he said, not sure whether he should be sad or happy.

"That is good," Raedfrith commented. "I suppose their magic is not stronger than ours. At least the bishop needs some kind of spell to keep him together with his horse. He is hardly a man to inspire respect among Saxons." He laughed loudly and strode across the enclosure to join the men.

"What do you know about this Christian fire, Ceda?" Luthwin asked. "Do we really need to fear fire if we do not yield to the bishop?"

The woman looked thoughtfully at him for a minute. "I do not know what this man said. But my grandmother did sometimes talk of a fire for the wicked folk. But she said it was only for Saxons and invaders. I am sorry, lad, that I know so little."

She glanced up quickly. At the same instant Luthwin also heard Wallen's laugh. The boy stood at the end of the enclosure among the slave huts, laughing at Brum, the village bully. The angry, somewhat older youth lunged once at Wallen, but Wallen backed away quickly, and Brum fell to his knees. Grinning, Wallen trotted toward the cook-shed. Brum got up and glared after him.

"If only my son would leave that rascal alone," Ceda murmured. "No good will come of getting him angry. He cannot bear to come out the loser."

Luthwin went to the hall for supper. Tonight he sat with his parents and Raedfrith. Carefully Hunwold explained to his wife all the bishop had said. She listened intently.

"Certainly you must go to Edwin yourself," she agreed. "Even a churlish man may speak the truth in some matters. You must find out for yourself from someone more trustworthy than he."

Hunwold finished the chunk of meat in his hand, wiped the grease from his fingers, and nodded. "I will begin preparations for the journey at once, and as soon as the harvest is secure and all the ceorls are free to protect the estates in my absence, I will leave. Winter will soon be upon us."

He turned to Luthwin. "How would you like to go with me, my son?"

Luthwin gasped. "To Edwin's court?"

"Of course," his father said. "You are old enough to learn the ways of men dealing with their lords. And I know you will honor your father by your behavior while you are there. You have good ears for listening, and you do not talk too much." He looked significantly at Raedfrith.

Luthwin saw his brother flush a deep red. Everyone knew how he had spoken out in the presence of the king of the Dalradian Scots. Hunwold had sworn that never again would Raedfrith go on such an important journey until he had learned more wisdom.

"I would like to go, Father," Luthwin said. "And I will be an honor to you before the king."

Hunwold gulped another cupful of mead. "Then it is decided. Your mother will instruct you in manners, for she herself lived at court in her youth."

Tonight Luthwin's head was as giddy as if he had been drinking mead again. While he lay in bed listening to the rain on the roof timbers, his mind whirled with plans. He was going to the court of King Edwin, ruler of all the Northumbrians and overlord of half of England.

Chapter Two

THROUGH DOWNS shrouded with fog the Saxon party traveled south. Hunwold insisted they must go even faster, pressed onward by some purpose more urgent than the question of the new religion, Luthwin guessed.

They took the ancient Roman road, crossed the Wall that long ago marked the northernmost part of Roman control, and forded the River Tyne. Ahead forests were wild and travelers few. They must pass close beside the stronghold of the Britons who remained in the lowlands. Luthwin felt the tension build up among his father's men when they rode by night under the oaks that blotted out any moonlight that might help them find their way. On either side he saw lights from villages, scattered and small, not defended with ramparts of wood the way the Saxons defended their tons.

York was like a new world to Luthwin. He marveled at the stone buildings and the remains of a city wall.

"This was a great center in Roman days," Hunwold told him. "The city still has a large number of Britons, who have been subdued into service. The king must be careful of their loyalty."

Luthwin looked at the arches and pillars around him. "I like our wooden houses better," he said. Somehow the stone seemed unfriendly and cold.

"It is against our blood to live in cities," his father said. "You see, even our king lives in a small villa away from the foreign buildings. He uses the city for his business, but he does not want to live inside stone walls left by another race of men."

Although Luthwin hoped they would stop long enough to see York, he saw only one building up close. Since it was stone and had no roof yet, he guessed it must be new.

"That is the house of worship for the Christian God," Hunwold commented. "The bishop's men from Rome are building it."

At York they left the River Swale. On the edge of the forest, near the broad sweep of marsh stretching to the north and to the sea, they found the royal villa.

The settlement was much larger than Hunwold's ton. Ramparts of earth and logs surrounded all the buildings. The great hall was magnificent. As they rode into the village, Luthwin looked up at the watchman sitting in his tower beside the gate. He felt sure that the guard could see visitors approaching from any direction for a great distance.

Sitting with the thanes who came with his father, Luthwin waited in the courtyard while Hunwold entered to speak to the king. The youth's eyes lingered on the rich clothing of the men who bustled about. A royal lady wearing scarlet and blue led two small boys and a little girl from the bower to the grand log house near the end of the only stone building in the enclosure. Luthwin wanted desperately to leave Twi and follow them—just to see inside such a big house.

A bell sounded inside the stone building. Several people came out, their heads bowed. Apparently used to visitors, they paid no heed to Luthwin and his father's men waiting on horseback. Last came a man wearing white robes. Another bishop, Luthwin thought. But the man was young and had a pleasant face. Maybe, Luthwin decided, his mother was right. Maybe all Christians were not so disagreeable as the one who had visited them on the Tweed.

That night the king gave Hunwold quarters in the log house. Luthwin had trouble sleeping in the heap of soft covers a servant brought him. A fire kept the room warm. By its flickering light he watched the hangings, stitched beautifully with birds and flowers, flutter against the walls. The gold fittings glittered when the flames licked higher, and up above he could see banners and flags swaying from the soot-blackened roof beams.

In the morning, he thought, I must remember to eat properly at the table the way mother told me. I must keep clean the whole time

I am here. He did not want to disgrace his family by seeming to be untrained in court manners. He wondered what kind of man the king was. Maybe tomorrow he would see.

But the next day it was not the king to whom a servant took him. Instead, the page introduced him to first one lady and then another. Finally he entered the warm, pleasant bower, low beside the wall of a larger building.

The room was fragrant and bright, with sun streaming in from windows open to the south. At the far end of the room a lady sat working. Everyone around him bowed. Self-consciously Luthwin tried to do the same thing. The woman nodded to him.

"Yes, bring him here," she commanded with a smile.

Luthwin liked her at once. Older than his own mother, she had her gray hair tucked carefully under a shimmering mantle as thin and sheer as a spider's web.

"So you are Hunwold's son?" she said. "Come here, lad, and talk with me." She waved the other women away and pointed to a stool near her. "Now we must get acquainted. Your father wishes you to stay with me for a time so that you may be educated. He says you are a bright boy, more sensible than his older son, and might profit from some study."

Luthwin gulped. "I would like that," he stammered, hardly able to imagine such a thing.

"My own son is studying his first Latin with one of the monks," she went on. "I want him to read the Holy Word for himself, and you must be able to do the same."

What did she mean? he wondered. Luthwin nodded politely at her words, but he did not understand.

"And, of course, you will learn the ways of court and the laws of our people, for you may someday be of service to your king and an honor to your father, although you are his youngest child."

She took a dainty pair of scissors from her workbox and cut a green thread. Carefully she knotted a golden one and drew it through her piece of linen.

He watched her face while she worked silently. So this, he thought, was the famous Aethelburh, the woman who had brought Christian missionaries to Northumbria and changed so many of the old ways.

Luthwin wondered how he could live at court, surrounded by so much grandeur. Could he always remember his manners, and how would he like to study every day? He remembered the hillside at home and his new sword. Would he have a chance to practice warfare? He was a Saxon. He needed to learn to handle a sword more than he needed to read a strange language.

Days passed before Luthwin met the king. Much secret activity had taken place. Messengers, soldiers, and even servants came stealthily to the settlement by night. Luthwin sensed that something was wrong. But the feast held in the great hall for the eorls made him forget the mystery for a while.

Under the hall's vast arches and oaken beams, tables spread with dishes of gold and silver reached from one end to the other. He had never smelled anything so wonderful. Glass bowls held bright fruits heaped high, and no commotion or loud talk went on there like that which occurred in Hunwold's hall.

At the head of the main table sat Edwin. The room glowed with his smile, but Luthwin felt that he was a strong man, as dangerous to an enemy as he was kind to his friends.

"My kinsmen and friends," the king said. "My house is honored. My heart is warmed and gladdened to share with you the wonderful bounty of my lands. Let us thank God for these blessings. Let us seek His aid in what we are about to do."

Luthwin looked at his father. Hunwold bowed his head in respect when the young priest prayed to the Christian God.

Up and down the table arose quiet talk. Luthwin listened. Some danger threatened the kingdom, he thought. They spoke only of the number of men they could collect and the arms they had stored.

He thought of Raedfrith's ring mail tunic. If his brother were here, he might get to use it. Would there be an invasion? Luthwin mused. What enemy had come so far south? He remembered his father going with his thanes and the ceorls from his own lands to push the Picts back across the River Tweed. And he remembered when Hunwold came home victorious. But Luthwin's oldest brother had died in one of the battles. The threat the nobles discussed must be a different kind of war. Hunwold would surely not be the leader. Edwin might himself lead his whole nation to battle.

After the feast Luthwin asked his father what was happening. Hunwold seemed unwilling to talk about it. "You will stay with the queen," he said. "I will send a messenger to tell your mother."

"Will you stay here, too?" Luthwin looked at the pile of his father's goods, apparently piled together in preparation for travel.

"No."

"I would rather go with you."

Hunwold thought for a moment. Luthwin watched his face, hoping.

"There is talk of an alliance between Cadwallon, of West Wales, and Penda, the prince of Mercia. They say that Edwin has no right to rule over them, and they intend to crush and destroy his kingdom."

"Does he have the right?" Luthwin asked.

"He who is strong enough to hold a kingdom together has the right to rule it," his father answered.

"Will they have a great army?" Suddenly Luthwin felt a cold lump in his stomach.

"Son, do not worry!" Hunwold slapped his son's back heartily. "Edwin has a still larger army than theirs, and his ships have subdued the coastline as far as the Isle of Man. We are men of war. We are not afraid of battle."

The boy grinned. "Then why do you not take me? I do not think I will learn to read. I saw a book in the queen's bower yesterday. It would take great magic to understand it."

"It takes understanding," his father contradicted. "Like all difficult tasks, you can do it if you use all your strength. You have a good mind, Luthwin. You must learn to read and write. You must learn the laws and customs that are becoming to one who rules."

In the days that followed, Luthwin saw little of his father. Someone rode home with a message to Luthwin's mother about his remaining at court. Men worked feverishly to gather arms and supplies and had no time to talk with a boy twelve years old and too young to help in battle. They thought only of battle, he mused. It was also about all he could think of.

The king and all but a few old men went to York, leaving the royal villa suddenly empty, silent. The bells in the little chapel rang morning and evening, their sound echoing through a deserted courtyard. Only court ladies and their children stood inside while the priest spoke in his strange language before the altar and chanted his low, musical rites.

During the day Luthwin sat with the young deacon James while he taught the king's little son and grandson. Even these small boys understood more than Luthwin did.

On a waxed tablet he practiced the letters James showed him. Finally he could write his own name. And when he saw the same simple words day after day, he could remember a few. But what good was that when he didn't know what they meant?

Used to being outdoors, he longed to be out on a meadow along the Tweed with Wallen, tumbling, wrestling, until they both lay exhausted, looking at the sky. He tried to make himself believe he was lucky to be at court. Neither of his brothers had even visited Edwin. Truthfully, he felt proud his father trusted him to remain there.

"Luthwin," Queen Aethelburh said one morning when she came to hear lessons, "you are learning letters. Are you learning the religion of Christ from your teacher?" She laid her hand on his shoulder, and he could not avoid her eyes. "That is my real reason for wanting you here. You would make a fine Christian."

Trembling inside, he looked at the copy of the Scriptures lying on the deacon's table. Was he learning her religion? He did not know anything about it yet—just a few words he could repeat.

The queen smiled. "Such promise you have!" She picked up his wax tablet and looked at his work. Luthwin could see her pleasure at what she saw. Still something clouded her eyes. "But what of the faith, Luthwin?" she repeated.

He tried to meet her steady eyes. "I know it means much to you," he said. "I do not know." Then he wondered if he should ask the one thing that did puzzle him. "Madam, what about the burning? The bishop said that unless we are baptized, we will burn in a terrible fire that never goes out."

"Wickedness must be destroyed," Queen Aethelburh said kindly. "If you hide the wickedness in your soul—But, come, Luthwin. Learn the words of life from the good deacon, and you will not need to fear."

Luthwin wanted to ask her what wickedness was. How could he avoid something he knew nothing about?

The deacon put his parchment aside. "He is a good student, madam. Do not be concerned. He learns readily. He works hard. And he will learn the true doctrines of the Holy Church as well. We must give him what time he needs. This religion is new to him, and it dawns slowly."

"Certainly," the queen said. "I did not mean to seem impatient."

Later Luthwin thought the visit over. He had told her the truth, he decided. He did not know enough to believe yet.

Guards now heavily patrolled the gates of the villa. The watchman shouted warnings whenever a visitor approached. And from the Mark far down the road, each visitor called out his name and business.

At York Edwin's forces gathered by the thousands. Daily supplies of food by cart and animal pack passed the villa. Luthwin knew that so large an army needed a great amount of food. It also impressed upon him the seriousness and size of the conflict.

Couriers carried news of ships bringing arms from the mainland and from the smiths of Ireland. The faces of passing soldiers mingled eagerness and strain. The battle would come. Everyone knew that. But Edwin's scouts had not discovered the enemy's location. To the south or to the west, in the moorlands or in the hills? Wherever they looked, the Mercians and the Britons had the advantage, many soldiers said, for throughout the land lived Britons enslaved by the Saxons. They would gladly help Cadwallon overcome their masters. Edwin would have no hope keeping his huge army a secret from his enemies. He could only wait and strike back when they met him at last.

"Cadwallon is a crafty leader," the son of another eorl told Luthwin. "He has done what no other Briton dared do since the Saxons came. He has found an ally among us. And that is most dangerous."

"But Penda is a fierce heathen," James the deacon interrupted. "That is the unnatural thing. Cadwallon, who claims to be a follower of Christ, of the old British church, has joined himself to one of another race and another religion."

"He is not particular what his allies believe or what color their hair is," the young man said. "Penda has chafed under Edwin's rule for a long time. He would be a king of importance himself if Edwin did not rule his lands better than he can."

Luthwin heard when Edwin moved his army out of York down the river. In the villa everyone expected news of the battle. A week passed. A messenger from Hunwold's estates brought news that Luthwin's brother Raedfrith had joined their father. Wallen came a day later with a cartful of supplies.

"Your mother says I am to stay with you," he told Luthwin. "She does not want you to be a burden to the king's household in this time of stress. And I am to work in the villa." He laughed, enjoying the idea.

"I am glad for that," Luthwin replied. "This place will not seem so strange with you here."

Even though the guards would not allow the boys outside the walls of the villa, he and Wallen could have games inside the courtyard, or even in his own chamber.

But they would have no chance for games. A herald bearing the king's colors raced into the villa that evening. The news he brought struck all of them speechless. Numb, they stood about the chapel door, trying to comfort one another. The queen closed herself and her children inside her rooms. Every servant wept unashamedly. Edwin was dead. The Northumbrians had scattered, those few hundred who had survived the battle at Heathfield. And now Penda and Cadwallon marched their savage army on York.

Luthwin pulled Wallen with him to the schoolroom behind the chapel. Feeling like a little boy again, needing someone to reassure him, he wanted to talk with James the deacon. Dread for his father and Raedfrith left him cold inside.

But the deacon was not there. A servant helped the bishop as he gathered a few things into a bag. "There is no reason to stay," the bishop said to no one in particular. "The hordes of heathen will be here, perhaps within another day. And they will not spare this sanctuary or its priest. They have no awe for holy things." His voice trailed off. Luthwin stepped back into the shadows, and the bishop did not see the two of them. He thrust a golden vessel used in the services into his already bulging bag.

The deacon came from the chapel then. "I will get your horse," he volunteered.

Luthwin and Wallen fell into step with him. "Will you go, too?" Luthwin asked.

The deacon shook his head. "I do not know where I will go, but I cannot leave all the people of Northumbria without spiritual help. The bishop is older. He is not willing to suffer the privations of difficult times. But God would not forgive me. I must stay somewhere nearby."

In the stables the servants saddled other mounts. "The queen is about to flee with the children," a groom explained. "She has an armed guard to take her to the court of her brother in Kent."

"But what will become of the villa?" Luthwin saw for the first time how helpless the small center was.

The groom shook his head. "We will each take what we can," he said.

The bishop left immediately. The queen with six ladies and their children gathered in the courtyard and mounted, ready to leave. An old thane from her guard helped her quiet the excited horse. Weeping, he waved his hand for silence.

"My dear people," Aethelburh said, struggling to suppress tears. "I have no choice but to leave you. I must save my husband's children. His name must not die. Each of you look to your own safety, for the enemy will sweep through the land, destroying and taking. You take first what you need for yourselves. Those of you who will be spared because of your race may stay here."

Her eyes found Luthwin in the crowd. "My child, you must reach your mother without harm. I commit you to the care of God. You must not wait for your father or his servants. Leave at once, and go by untraveled ways."

A choked sob caught in Luthwin's throat. Around him the people pressed toward the queen, but her soldiers held them back. Slowly the train of horses left the enclosure, threading its way across the rim of dry ground at the edge of the marsh.

From his chamber Luthwin brought his cloak, a blanket, and his sword. Wallen had Twi and a horse from the royal stable ready, a large bag hanging from each saddle. "I came by the coast," he said. "We had better go back that way. It will be safer than striking through territory we do not know."

He patted the strange horse. With a nervous whinny it trotted out the gate, Twi following.

Darkness hung like a shroud in the cloudy sky, waiting for sunset to cover everything. But Luthwin urged Twi to keep up with Wallen's bigger horse. They must go as far as they could on the old paved road tonight. They must reach the sea.

"This is far from York," Luthwin finally announced. "There will be no Britons knowing about Edwin's defeat this soon."

Wallen rubbed his knuckles into his horse's mane, for his hands were cold. He looked back the way they had come, at the desolate marshes on either side. "We will not worry about anything but going a long way tonight. No one is after us. Who could find two boys in all this land if we tried to keep out of sight?"

His chuckle made Luthwin feel better. The observation was true. But a haunting question still burned in the Saxon boy's heart.

"Do you think Hunwold lived through the battle?" His mouth trembled, and he saw that Wallen did not want to answer. "How long will it take us to reach the Tweed?" He would force himself to keep his mind off his father and brother. He would need all his wits to get home safely himself.

The slave boy shrugged. "Five days, I think. We hurried when we came from the north. Some places we had to be careful, even on this road."

Luthwin remembered coming south on the Great Road. He knew what Wallen meant. At the same time he wondered how long it would take for all the Briton farmers perched in their tiny huts on the hilltops to find out about their kinsmen's victory. When they knew, a traveling Saxon would have no safety. He and his friend were on their own now until they reached Hunwold's estate. They would not dare ask for shelter at a cottage along the way.

Suddenly Luthwin felt hungry. At noon he had eaten a lot at the villa. But that was hours ago. The dark and the cold and the excitement left him famished. Not a single oat cake nestled in the pocket of his tunic.

"Why did I forget food?" he muttered. "I never thought of it."

"I did," Wallen said. He clucked for his pony to stop, then patted the bag hanging in front of him. "I found plenty in the queen's larder. And I did just what she said. I took what we would need."

They got off their horses. An overcast moon had burst through a thin place in the clouds. Sitting on the ground, they ate bread and dried meat. In a few minutes they were moving again. Just before dawn the road rose out of the marshy land into forest, giving them enough cover to rest.

In the afternoon Luthwin awoke. A soft rain pattered on the leaves of the oaks, crisped by frost and hanging lifeless on the boughs. He pulled his blanket closer about his neck and looked through the trees.

The bright green of mistletoe dotted the upper branches of one oak shattered by lightning. It hung in patches as fresh as the first new heather leaves in spring, as if it did not feel winter threatening in every cold wind off the sea.

I wonder if there is anything to that old belief about mistletoe, Luthwin mused. How could a soul of the tree live in the tough little plant when the oak died? But then, when he thought about death, he wondered if any man could tell what really did happen to dead people.

He shuddered. What if Hunwold or Raedfrith had died with Edwin at Heathfield? Was his father even now burning in the terrible fire that never went out as the bishop threatened he would? Or had he gone to the Saxon warriors' land of drunken pleasure and ease?

Luthwin remembered seeing an eorl buried once with a boat and a sword and a spear and much gold. They said he would need such things if he traveled far in the other world.

Wallen stirred.

"We should get started," Luthwin said. The Celtic boy rubbed his face and brushed rain from his hair. He pulled a sack open, took out an apple for himself, and gave one to Luthwin.

"We will go through rough land today," he said. "There are downs and woods so thick you can get lost in daylight."

Now they had no road, just a trail worn in the grass where people traveled often. For the first time Luthwin wondered about the people who lived in England in the dim past. Until then he had always taken the high, firm roads for granted as if they existed there naturally like the hills or rivers. His father said Saxons did not use Roman cities or stone buildings. But always they used the roads. Maybe the roads had helped the Saxon conquer the land, he thought.

Chapter Three

ALL DAY they rode close enough to the sea to hear breakers hitting the beach. Sometimes Luthwin felt they went far enough up and down over the rough hills to equal the distance they traveled toward home.

He was sure they were in Saxon country. On the slopes along streams they saw tons much like Hunwold's, surrounded by fields and pastureland. Herds of cattle grazed the barren lands too stony for the plow. Here, Luthwin thought, they might safely seek shelter if they really had to have it.

The next day they reached the River Tees. But the boys could find no bridge or ford. The river, flooded from days of rain, spread across the low country, rushing and swirling until it emptied into the bay.

"We will have to follow it upstream," Luthwin said with a sigh.

Wallen looked ruefully up the river. "We crossed here on a raft. Some men taking supplies to the army had camped here with a raft they had made to carry their things across."

Luthwin scanned the surface of the water in both directions. Nothing but a few birds dipping to catch minnows caught his eye. He saw no one at all on either side of the river.

By night they reached a Saxon ton. Luthwin began to wonder how far they would have to follow the Tees before they found a place to cross.

"I think we should stop here," he told Wallen, remembering the rule of hospitality that seemed almost a religion with his people. The Saxons never turned away a stranger who came in friendship. At the ton's Mark he shouted, then waited for an answer. Only the distant chattering of a bird broke the silence.

"Maybe they did not hear you," Wallen suggested. His plowboy shout echoed across the meadow from the hillside. But no one came out of the ton, and still no one answered.

"Shall we go in?" The Celtic slave stood beside his nervous horse, searching the fields for a sign of someone coming home late from working.

"Yes, but be careful," Luthwin warned. "You know the law. A stranger who does not sound his horn before entering a ton—"

But they had no horn to blow. Slowly they approached the enclosure.

Wallen stopped. "I smell something."

Luthwin looked where he pointed. A thin circle of smoke hung over the ton—smoke not from a cooking fire. "It smells like dung and feathers," he said. At once he understood.

Wallen went ahead cautiously. "They burn everything, then leave."

He stopped where the gate hung crooked, broken by the blows of axes. "I do not see a person inside," he whispered. "Should we go in?"

Charred black roof beams sagged to the floors of the gutted bowers. Raindrops glistened on the burnt timbers. The great hall was a skeleton of oak beams against the twilight sky. It was the stables they smelled, Luthwin decided.

"What happened to the people?" he asked. "Should we see if we can find anyone who needs our help?"

His friend shook his head and laughed bitterly. "If anyone remained behind, you can do them no good. My kinsmen do a good job!"

Luthwin looked at him. Did Wallen side with the enemy? Could he be trusted? The two of them had played together since childhood. Although Ceda was a slave, Luthwin loved her almost as much as he loved his own mother. Still, they were Celts, Britons. Maybe they too felt a loyalty to their own race stronger than any friendship. If he met a band of the enemy now, what would Wallen do?

With a shiver Luthwin turned Twi around. "I do not want to stay here. It smells just like death itself."

Wallen rode behind him down the path to the road they had left along the river. In silence they went on into the night.

His mind occupied, Luthwin did not hear the noise until Wallen stopped. The Celt turned his ear to the wind and listened. "I think we are coming to another settlement."

"I hear it, too. They must have a large herd of cattle." Luthwin tried to sort out the many sounds. "I hear cows, I think."

But human voices mixed with the bellowing. Everyone in the settlement should have been sleeping now, for it was nearly midnight. The two youths rounded a curve in the road. Through the trees Luthwin saw a fire, blazing high and surrounded by at least a hundred men. "Stop!" he whispered. "It must be the raiding band!"

He tried to think what they should do. Wallen pulled his horse close beside his.

"Can we get around them if we do not make a sound?" Luthwin asked, feeling a tingling race down his back. He wanted to try. His hand caressed his sword's ornamented hilt. He might need that sword—he might use it yet tonight!

Stealthily Wallen slid to the ground from his horse. Luthwin led Twi behind him, unable to keep from smiling to himself. With all the noise the soldiers made, the invaders would probably not hear a whole troop of soldiers passing. Still he must keep outside the glow of their fire. Someone might be alert and watching.

Carefully moving a step at a time, they edged around the campfire. It had rained off and on for several days. The damp ground contained no dry twigs to betray them with a snap or crack under a careless foot. Their feet sank deep into the moss and short grasses.

At last trees surrounded them again, the Briton raiders behind them.

They mounted. "We made it!" Wallen slapped his horse's neck. The horse lunged ahead, surprised. On the wet earth he slipped, whinnying in alarm, and the Celtic slave jumped free of the saddle as the animal fell.

"Ho!" someone shouted on the road ahead of them. "Who is that?"

"Not one of our band for sure," his companion answered. "Here! I see two lads on horseback."

Out of the darkness hands grabbed the reins of Luthwin's horse. A flickering light fell around him. Not stopping to think, he jumped. Headlong he ran through the tangle of brush with only the sound of his friend crashing through the undergrowth to lead him. Behind him a torch swayed in an unsteady hand. The two Britons shouted to the others celebrating around the fire. Panic gripped Luthwin. If the whole troop joined the search, what chance would he and Wallen have to get away?

His sword swung at his side. Its thump against his leg almost matched the pounding of his heart as he heard the noise of soldiers taking up the hunt. Now he could hear no sound of Wallen ahead. Had the Celt left him, to side with the enemy? The searchers closed behind him.

Like a blind man, Luthwin plunged on. A rotting log caught his foot and headlong he sprawled into the wet ground. He scrambled to his knees in an instant, but not soon enough. He could hear someone shuffling about on either side. Behind him torchlight flickered on the boughs.

He flattened, crawled on his stomach, and stretched along the low side of the log that had tripped him, hardly daring to breathe. The log vibrated as a soldier crashed into it. With a volley of oaths, the Briton stopped to rub his shins, bending near enough for Luthwin to touch him if he wanted to reach out.

"He was over here," another man shouted. "I hear something moving."

"How can you hear a thing with all the noise you make shouting?" retorted the first soldier. "But why worry ourselves? We have their horses. The horses are worth more to us than the lads are. Besides, they cannot get far. We have all the fords now, and there is another band of Britons a few miles ahead of us."

"I agree," someone else mumbled. "Let's go back to camp. I was in the middle of drinking my mead. One does not find such good Saxon mead every day." He laughed loudly.

"They were just boys," the first soldier said, stumbling back toward the path.

At last Luthwin dared to fill his lungs. Trembling, he lay on the chilling ground for hours, afraid that if he left in the darkness he would make so much noise that he would arouse the Britons again.

When he could see the dim shapes of the trees around him, he got up slowly, every bone aching with cold. He followed the slope of the land to the river. In the shadow of the trees he walked along in the tall grass, watchful for any sight of Wallen. An intermittent drizzle soaked his clothing, and water trickled through his long hair and down his face.

Once he saw footprints in the soft earth and realized he was also leaving tracks. As cold as he was, he began to walk in the water, worried that someone might try to follow him. Numbness reached up his legs.

He wondered how far he would have to walk along the river. And if he did come to a ford, how could he cross? Would there be men guarding it, ready to capture any Saxon foolish enough to show himself? If he could only stop his minds endless questioning.

At last he sat down on a log to rest. A wind had come up, he noticed, making the damp air feel even colder. He was wet and hungry. A fish hawk dipped to the surface of the water, coming up with a flopping fish. He mused about the possibility of catching some fish himself, but he had no way of doing it. And he had no fire. The thought of uncooked fish did not stir his appetite, terribly hungry as he was.

When it got dark, he slept where he was, pulling his knees against his chest to hold his body heat. He woke in the morning feeling stiff. Looking through the boughs at the sky, he felt a faint gladness that the clouds were at last breaking up. Today it would not rain, a small comfort.

During the second day alone, he heard men passing on the road. By now he felt certain that they no longer looked for him. He stopped to listen as they went by. The babble of their voices told him nothing but that they had been doing more drinking than fighting. He wondered if they were the same men that he and Wallen had circled two nights before.

Later he came to an opening where only a few feet separated the road and the river. Across a low meadow he saw the ruins of another ton, still smoking. I might find something to eat here, he thought aloud. He watched for a long time to be sure that no one was inside.

He could see that the Britons had taken what they wanted and set fire to anything left. But with all the rain of the past week, the fire had not finished its work. All about lay signs of the struggle that went on while the villagers fought to save their lives. Luthwin tried not to see. He must find food. That was the important thing.

I am the son of a warrior, he reminded himself. I must get used to the sight of bloodshed before I am allowed to go to battle myself.

He closed his eyes when he passed the back entrance of the women's building. Inside there might be something left.

The roof had only partly burned, the damp rushes hanging in charred bunches through the beams. The Britons had pulled the rich draperies from their places, and the bare walls showed through the tangled remains. He crossed the room, ready to open the ax-scarred door.

Footsteps clattered on the loose stones on the other side. Quickly Luthwin slipped behind a ripped but still hanging tapestry, pulled his sword out of its sheath, and waited.

Creaking, the door opened. Someone stood behind it, checking every detail before he came in. Luthwin could see only a hand resting on the broken shaft of a spear. The person hesitated, listening. Did he hear his breathing? Luthwin wondered. The Saxon youth felt his pulse throbbing at the roots of his hair.

The door opened farther. The person behind it chuckled, confident the room was empty.

A wave of relief washed over Luthwin. "Wallen!" he cried, dashing out. He seized his friend by both hands, laughing and crying, trying to talk. But only unintelligible sounds came out.

"You are here for the same reason I am," Wallen guessed. "I have looked around half the day hoping to find enough to last us till we get home. I have some dried fish and some raisins so far. And I did find some warm clothes for you, Luthwin. Come on with me."

He had a few things stacked in the corner of the cookshed. "There is still dry wood here," he explained. "And no one will suspect a thing if they see smoke rising from this ruined place."

"You found a blanket!" Luthwin fingered the singed edges. Though coarse and smelling of smoke, it at least was dry.

They laid a fire in the hearth, starting the blaze with bits of still-smoldering wood from the stable. Luthwin watched Wallen stir the dried fish into boiling water.

"Where did you find that little cooking pot?"

The Celt pointed across the courtyard. "I think it was a toy. It was in a child's room. The raiders hardly touched anything there, but the fire spoiled most of it."

While the food cooked, Wallen brought out the clothes. "I think these will fit you, Luthwin," he said. "They are not as fine as the ones your mother makes for you, but they are not torn like the ones you are wearing now." He laid a peasant's outfit on the end of the stone hearth and grinned back at his master's son.

"I am bigger, so I get these. And I will be dressed better than I have been all my life—better than I will ever dress again." Luthwin stared at the suit of red wool his friend held up. Its tunic reached to Wallen's knees. Fine embroidery decorated the leggings and cloak.

Luthwin smiled and picked up the peasant leggings. "You planned to find me then?" The outfit the slave youth had given Luthwin was too obviously small for Wallen to have ever intended to wear it himself.

"Find you?" Wallen's face showed surprise. "Why shouldn't I find you? I had to find you!"

"But you are a Briton," Luthwin began. "You would have no trouble going anywhere you want. You are dark and ruddy, like most of your people. No one would mistake you for a—"

The other boy's face turned red with anger. "You must never say that again!" His voice shook. "Do you understand? I am a Celt, and I am proud of my race. But my people have ruined the land and maybe even killed part of your family. You are my friend. Your family is mine. Your enemy is mine. Do you understand?" He ended in a tense whisper.

Luthwin nodded.

Turning away from him, Wallen said, "Put on those dry clothes."

Luthwin obeyed, his heart singing. Wallen was loyal. Why had he doubted his friend? The Celtic boy had never seemed like a slave to him. Hunwold said he treated him like a brother. And it was true. It was how he felt toward Wallen.

They slept warm beside the hearth under the blanket that night.

"We might as well stay here a few days," Wallen suggested in the morning. "By then the raiding parties will have moved farther along the river, and we can travel more safely."

The Saxon youth agreed. "Did you hear what the soldier said? They have all the fords."

"That may be true, and it may not be," Wallen replied. "A Briton is likely to exaggerate if he is in the mood for it."

A lone hen scratched in the straw pile. On the far side, next to the enclosure wall, the boys found a nest with five eggs. When they became hungry, Wallen fixed the eggs. Their search also turned up six loaves of hard bread in the end of the cookshed.

They spent a long time in the great hall. Luthwin stared at the sagging beams overhead. Shattered earthenware dishes covered the long oaken table. They rummaged through the rubble on the floor. Luthwin held up a tin vessel, then opened it. It smelled sour from old mead.

Wallen found a knife blade without a handle and an empty scabbard. He hooked the scabbard to his belt and thrust the blade into it as far as it would go. "It is too wide to fit," he said, "but I will keep it. I can make a handle of bone."

Before dark they ate more bread and some broth. Almost ready to settle down for the night, Luthwin suddenly laid down the armful of straw he was spreading on the stone floor. "I think I hear horses coming." He looked out the gate.

Already a group of riders galloped across the meadow from the river and the road.

"They must be looking for some dry firewood," Wallen muttered. "Where can we hide our things?"

They did not have time to move them far. Hurriedly they dragged everything behind the storehouse. While the Britons swaggered into the enclosure, the boys stealthily moved their supplies to the loft.

The soldiers did not bother to search the ruined ton. Instead, they dragged dry wood to the center of the courtyard and started a fire. After tying their horses, one man pulled back a layer of wet hay from the stack and fed them. Then the men grouped around the fire to get warm.

In the loft of the storehouse Luthwin and Wallen inched forward until they could see everything from a crack between the logs. Luthwin pointed to the heap of goods the men had piled on the ground. "They were certainly busy today," he whispered.

Swaggering in the firelight, the Britons hung gold and silver objects around their necks. "Now we have our share," one boasted. "We can start for home. And my wife will think she is a queen with fine linens to wear and a silk mantle."

"This day has treated us well, indeed," another soldier replied. He held up a sword and two small silver spoons. "When our companions left us here yesterday morning, they did not know we had the most lucky find in store for us. This villa was but trash compared with what we found by staying one more day. Do you agree, my friends?"

"Aye!" several grunted.

A handful of men left the fire and dug into a pile of loot. The leader came back holding a gold cup that shone in the firelight. He showed it around. "But whose will this be?" he cried. "So rich a prize does not belong just to the first man to lay his hands on it. It belongs to us all."

"We all risked our lives in this venture," someone agreed.

One man stood up, waving his arms. "I say it is mine. He who takes a piece of ivory or glassware can keep it. He who finds gold may keep it, too!"

A murmur of disagreement passed over the group.

"It came from a holy place. It must be treated with more respect."

A booming laugh interrupted the speaker. "A Saxon chapel a holy place?"

Recognizing the voice, Luthwin gripped Wallen's shoulder. "That is the one that got our horses!" He strained to see better. If it was the same man, Twi must be around the corner with the other horses.

"We will get them back!" Wallen whispered emphatically. Luthwin could sense a plan shaping itself in his friend's mind.

Below in the courtyard the Britons used some kind of lot or gambling device to decide who should get the golden cup. Their attention occupied, they would be less likely to notice the boys moving about.

"Shall we go now or later?" Luthwin asked.

The Celt looked through the door at the back of the loft. "The moon will not come up for hours yet tonight. It will be too dark once their fire dies down. The horses are around the building from the men. We can reach them without the soldiers seeing us."

"But how can we get everything out?" Luthwin said, glancing at the pile of food.

"Do you think we can get it over the wall here?" Wallen wiggled a plank loose and slid it out the door to the top of the barricade. "Try that. You are not as heavy as I am."

The Saxon stepped on the plank.

"Is it steady enough?"

"There is a lot of spring in it. But I think I can balance all right."

Wallen drew a cord from his tunic. He bent a piece of tin into a hook, tying it to the cord. Luthwin walked across the plank to the top of the barricade and caught the rope when Wallen threw it. In minutes they had dropped all their supplies to the outside of the wall. After a quick look from the loft to see if the Britons were still in the courtyard, they ran between the barricade and the sheds to the stable.

"Do you see our horses?" Wallen hissed between his teeth.

Luthwin shook his head. In the dim firelight playing on the haystacks he could see nearly fifty horses eating. He did not see Twi. Glancing past the end of the stable, he saw that the soldiers still argued about some of the booty. Two men were talking to each other as they walked around, but he could see they often approached the fire to hear the argument going on there.

Feeling like a shadow as he moved slowly, bent almost double, Luthwin reached the haystacks. He wondered if the horses would give his presence away. An old bay raised its head. The boy patted its shoulder, whispering reassurance. Two smaller horses stood together, tied to a rail. A young mare tossed her mane and snorted.

"What is the matter with the horses?" a Briton shouted.

As if in answer, another horse kicked the mare, and she snorted again. Luthwin froze beside a post.

Another soldier laughed. "Just a friendly quarrel," he said. "You cannot put a bunch of strange animals together and expect them to be better friends than their former masters have been."

For a few minutes Luthwin waited. Then the men went back to a game they had marked on the ground. He moved down the line of horses until he saw Twi. Gently he circled the horse's neck with his arms. "Quiet, boy. I have come to get you." He unfastened the rope. Like a puppy glad to see his master, Twi followed him.

The other horses screened them until Luthwin stood at the corner of the stable again. He waited for the game to break up. Everyone began praising the winner. Amid the shouting he dashed across the open space. No one seemed to notice the clatter of Twi's hooves on the hard earth.

"Wonderful!" Wallen slapped Luthwin's back. "Now see if I can be so lucky getting the other one." While the noise still filled the courtyard, Wallen slipped to the stable. The horses seemed uneasy, restless. Luthwin watched his friend move with caution, stopping often to see if the soldiers looked his way. It would take him longer. His horse was not an old friend like Twi. It shied from Wallen as it would from any other stranger. The slave youth would have to coax him a step at a time.

The men paid no attention when a colt whinnied. A stallion kicked viciously. Luthwin drew a deep breath as Wallen dodged the animal's heels just in time. Gripping the rope close to his horse's head to keep it from bolting, Wallen patted its neck until it calmed again.

Luthwin glanced at the Britons. Outlined by the flickering firelight, they bent in a ring around the game, watching every move the players made. Luthwin signaled to Wallen. Moving slowly, his friend led the horse across the opening.

Luthwin breathed a deep breath of relief and grinned. "Now we just have to make it out the gate."

Wallen started leading his horse back behind the buildings, and Luthwin tugged on Twi's rope. Their steps, cushioned by the fallen thatching, were as silent as a passing rabbit.

The Saxon boy suddenly realized how close to the gate the Britons stood. When he stopped with Wallen at the end of the shed, he stood near enough to hear the clink of the tiny dice on the stones and the low murmur of the players begging their gods for luck. He knew he could control Twi, but would Wallen's horse stand patiently, waiting for just the chance they needed to escape?

Chapter Four

THE BRITONS tired of the game, Luthwin noticed. One by one they turned away, some to gather straw for sleeping, some to have one more drink of stolen mead.

"Better toss a bit more feed to the horses, Reud," the leader of the band shouted.

A burly soldier obeyed. Luthwin listened. He heard the rustle of hay and the sound of horses stamping.

"Will he notice?" Wallen whispered the question in his ear.

Twi was the only light-colored one in the herd. The soldier would surely notice its absence. Luthwin carefully judged the distance to the gate. "We will have to try for it now!"

Wallen nodded, but he then looked back with a look of horror.

Luthwin saw the giant Reud gripping his friend by the arm. Without a word, Reud shoved Wallen ahead of him back toward the stable. For an instant Luthwin wanted to run, but he could not leave Wallen now. With one rueful look at the gate, he followed with Twi.

Reud took the ropes of both horses. "Now, lads," he said, "you could not get away with everybody sitting around the gate like that, could you?" He looked at them squarely.

With a thrill of hope Luthwin noticed that his voice held a note of friendliness even though his manner was rough.

"Lads, do you think you could get away with it? I saw the two of you slipping like ghosts among the horses. I did. And I said to myself, 'Those lads have a lot of pluck to take their ponies from under our noses.' So I did not let anyone guess what I saw. You will have to leave the rest to me."

He smiled, and Luthwin's heart trembled. The smile seemed to hold both a promise and a threat. He did not know what to think of the huge Briton.

Reud tied the halter ropes to a post. "Just stay here with the horses, both of you. And I will see that you make it out as soon as you can."

"We will need a good head start to keep ahead of the raiding band tomorrow," Luthwin said.

"You will get a generous lead."

The Briton made a lot of noise feeding the other horses, stamping his feet, clattering the pavement with his fork. Then like an ungainly ox moving about its stable, he walked across the courtyard and joined his companions. The men's voices murmured across the flickering shadows.

Luthwin sat down on a heap of straw. "Do you think we can really trust him?"

Wallen chuckled. "I suppose we have to trust him, Luthwin. He knows we are here now."

"We could go over the wall," Luthwin suggested. "We do not have to take the horses."

"I say we should take a chance on him," Wallen said. He fingered the hem of his tunic, thinking. "Without the horses we will have trouble fording the river. And we will be able to carry little on our backs. This Reud is a rough fellow, but he does have some kindness in him."

Luthwin stretched out on a dry place in the straw. He knew he could never sleep, but he needed to rest. Wallen was right, he supposed. At least they would wait and see.

Near midnight Reud appeared suddenly beside them. "I am the only one awake," he muttered. "Now go as quietly as you did before. I will be around by the gate in case you need me to help." He glanced quickly at the smoldering fire. "And if you need to cross the river, I will be at the next ford tomorrow night. Keep out of sight. I will find you."

Luthwin led Twi to the gate. In minutes he and Wallen stood outside it, loading their supplies.

By dawn they had ridden miles down the road. Travel would be more dangerous in the daylight, Luthwin thought, but they could walk along the water parallel to the road. Ahead the river straightened. All the way across broken stone pillars showed where an ancient bridge had stood.

"I know where we are!" Luthwin exclaimed. "My father came this way when we went to see Edwin. This is where the Great Road crosses the River Tees."

Already they saw signs of activity. Band after band of Britons rode into the water. Only in the middle of the stream did their horses have to swim, and the current did not seem to be strong now.

"The water is lower than when my father crossed," Luthwin said, getting off Twi.

He led his horse to a bush and tied him where he could feed on the tall grass, unseen by the men in the water upstream. Wallen pulled food from his bag, and they ate, always alert for the sound of someone approaching.

Most of the day they slept, knowing that if they crossed at night with Reud to help them, they would spend the entire night on the move.

At dusk Luthwin loaded his things on Twi. They had no way of knowing when Reud would come or if he would find them as he promised. But they were close enough to the road, Luthwin thought, as close as they dared to go.

"This is the eighth day since we left Edwin's villa," Wallen said, looking across the water, which still reflected sunset colors. "I was wrong about how long the journey would take us. I should have expected some trouble."

Luthwin munched the dry bread he held. "We have still a great distance to go. Do you think the Great Road will be safe this far north?"

Wallen shrugged. "Is there any place that is safe now?"

"While Edwin reigned, men said even a mother with a new born baby could safely walk the kingdom from one end to the other," Luthwin mused.

"We could go much faster on the road." Wallen's brow furrowed. "It might be worth the chance."

"If the road just went through forest instead of downs—"

The Saxon youth paused. "I hear a band of men coming." He listened. There was no mistake. He could pick out several voices that had become familiar while he and Wallen hid in the ruined ton. "I wonder what they stole today," he whispered. He tried to see them as they passed on the other side of a dense tangle of brush.

The men went by and stopped where another group had settled for the night.

In the darkness every leaf that fell sounded a warning to Luthwin. When a squirrel jumped from its nest to another tree, he went weak from momentary fright. "I wish Reud would hurry," he said. "I am as nervous as a colt."

Wallen leaned against his horse and yawned. "I keep thinking I hear someone coming, but I guess my ears are playing tricks." He laughed softly. Luthwin wished he could be as relaxed.

The raiding band did not cross the ford when they finished eating around the big campfire. Instead, they set out south on the Great Road. In a few minutes the last rattle of their booty against their saddles died away, and the whole forest fell empty of sound.

Then Luthwin heard footsteps. At once Wallen leaned forward, listening. Back and forth they sounded on the packed trail. Every few steps the walker stopped.

"Saxons?" It came as hardly more than a whisper.

Wallen's fingers dug into Luthwin's shoulder.

"Saxons?" The voice was nearer.

It was Reud, Luthwin knew.

"We are here," the youth replied softly.

"Come out, lads. But do not make much noise." A horse snorted somewhere not far off.

"We can come along the water—easier to follow the shore in the darkness," Wallen said. "Should we do that?"

"Yes, along the water." Reud cleared his throat. "I will go around to the ford myself to meet you. I gave the guards something to keep them busy for a while." He laughed. "Still you had better come as quietly as you can."

Reud climbed on an enormous black stallion—a darker shadow against the night—when they reached the fording place, and waved for them to come after him. He waded the horse straight across, close to the pillars. Luthwin clung low against Twi's back, encouraging him where he had to swim in the middle of the river.

On the other side they came out with their clothes wet up above the knees. Cold as he felt, Luthwin looked back with relief to see the river gleaming faintly behind him.

"Now," Reud began. "You owe me something for my trouble."

"But we have—"

The man waved his hand to interrupt Luthwin. "Not gold. I have found my share of gold these past days." He coughed and mumbled something Luthwin could not understand. "I have reason to make a journey north. If we travel together, there will be safety for you, and certain, ah advantages for me." He leaned forward in his saddle, trying to see them better in the dim moonlight. "Will you accept that?"

Luthwin thought it over. "We will need to go by the Great Road. Are you going that way?"

"Perhaps, if it is not too busy. But is this agreed? You will not try to escape? You will not run off while you think I sleep? Is that a fair price for my help?"

"We will stay with you at least until we reach the Wall," Luthwin promised.

"Then we must start." Without another word, Reud set off. His black stallion kept the smaller horses at a trot. Exhausted at dawn, Luthwin wondered how many miles they had covered since crossing the river.

But during the following days he began to respect the Briton's cunning. At night they camped, always near enough to the road to hear anyone passing, yet concealed themselves. Reud seemed to have a special sense about danger. Often he led them into a small ravine out of sight just minutes before a party of strangers passed. He seemed to fear nothing—and saw everything.

On the third day they reached the Roman Wall. Crumbling into its earthworks, it stretched to the east and to the west over rugged downs.

Reud pointed to a fallen stone tower with grass growing over the heap of rocks marking the site of a former settlement. "My ancestors belonged to the legion that built that camp." Luthwin noticed he sat a little straighter on his horse. "They were of the bravest men in the Roman army. For a hundred years they kept the Picts and Scots beyond the Wall until the Empire fell."

He waved his arm to take in the whole horizon. "We were Romans in those days. Below the Wall a Briton was a citizen of the world empire, with all the rights of any man alive. Not a slave among us. All free men. And look at us now!" His voice rose with bitterness, and his hands whitened from gripping the reins. "A few hundred families holed up in the hills where Saxons do not want to bother with the thin, rocky soil—coming down at the risk of our lives and all we have." For a while he remained silent, riding with eyes straight ahead.

Luthwin looked at Wallen and wondered what he was thinking about. Somehow he had never thought of Britons as anything but servants. His friend raised his eyebrows as if asking a question. Apparently Wallen also wondered if they had made a mistake in accepting Reud's help.

The big man slumped back to his usual position in the saddle. His body swayed with the rhythm of his horse's steps. He seemed half asleep. When he spoke again, it startled Luthwin. "Lads, how does it happen that you two are traveling together like brothers, one of you a flaxen-haired fellow and the other a true Celt?"

"We came from the same estate," Luthwin began. "Wallen's family has served there for a long time."

The Briton looked at him with disbelief. "And you played with a slave?"

Luthwin nodded. "Wallen brought supplies and came to help in the villa where I went to study." He caught himself. Had he said too much already?

"And we fled together," Wallen finished. "I go where he goes. He would do the same for me."

Reud nodded. "I know of that kind of loyalty. Yes, it is often stronger than other relationships. Perhaps it is not so rare a thing as I thought." He paused. "But tell me now. Are you from the northern province of Bernicia then?"

"From the very border," Luthwin said proudly. "My father has held the River Tweed for twenty years for Northumbria."

"Ah, Hunwold!"

"Do you know him?" Luthwin gasped. He saw the Briton's face harden.

"I know him." Reud pushed up his sleeve. A long red wound, just now healing, stretched from his wrist to his elbow. "And he has reason to remember me." A look of fierceness glazed his eyes.

Then my father is still alive! Luthwin thought. He burned to ask more but did not dare. Already he had said enough to cause trouble for himself and Wallen.

They did not take the Great Road north. Instead Reud led them west along the Wall that day and the next. In the lowlands they joined another highway. On it they went north at last, but the country was wild and strange. Through uplands covered with heather the horses plodded day after day. Luthwin realized that he and Wallen were prisoners now. He wanted to talk with Wallen, but they had no chance with Reud's sharp eyes watching them constantly.

He did not even hope they could escape the huge Briton while they traveled. Reud never really slept. His ears caught the faintest sound in the night. And all day he kept his black at such a pace they had to hurry to keep up. Lagging would leave them to the mercy of his anger.

I do not think he planned to let us go home even before he knew that Hunwold is my father, Luthwin mused once. He has some reason for taking us along. Maybe he will use us for hostages to ensure his own safety in Saxon territory. But when he considered the possibility, Luthwin realized that they had already gone beyond Saxon settlement and far to the west. He thought of the possibility that Reud might sell them as slaves. The Dalradian Scots would pay more than the Picts would. And since Reud could not try to force a ransom from Hunwold, he might peddle them to the slave traders. If only they could find out the nature of his business in the north. By now Luthwin had traveled more than two hundred miles from his home.

Luthwin's eyes swept the country, always searching. He did not know what he expected to see. On the hills sheep and goats fed, and in the valleys or on southern slopes small cottages hugged the side of a bank, their thatched roofs blending with the tufts of grass growing around them.

Each day grew a little colder than the one before. One afternoon snow began to fall. The snowfall forced Reud to seek shelter inside a cottager's smoky, filthy home.

"We will travel only two more days," Reud told them in the morning when they faced the biting wind, straight out of the north. "And if the cold is still bad tonight, we will keep moving. I cannot afford hospitality that demands another of my gold pieces."

The cold did not let up. By dusk snow covered the hillsides, but even through the clouds a full moon lit the way for them. Luthwin pushed his hands inside the sleeves of his peasant's shirt to keep them warm and let Twi go on his own.

Short and surefooted, the horse was used to winter travel. Now and then when his feet began to slide, he caught his balance again and plodded ahead. Luthwin wondered if Twi shared his hunger. He could feel the horse's ribs against his legs. There had been little for him to eat on the hurried ride north.

At daylight they entered the head of a valley and threaded their way along a stream through a narrow gorge. In an hour Luthwin could hear breakers beating the seashore. Ahead stone buildings resembling beehives clung to the rocks near the water's edge.

"You, lads, come with me," Reud ordered. He dismounted and disappeared inside the nearest hut.

Luthwin was surprised when he came into the small room. Unlike the shepherd's cottage, it was clean. A peat fire smoked on a hearth in the center. The column of smoke found its way through a tiny hole in the point of the roof. The hut had no windows.

"I have come to see Oswald, the prince of Bernicia," Reud addressed a wrinkled woman sitting on a cushion beside the fire. "I am Reud from Scots Dyke on the River Tees."

The woman looked at him with penetrating eyes. "I will send a messenger," she said after a pause. "You will have to wait." She stood up and walked with halting steps to the door, waved to someone outside, and returned to her seat.

Reud cleared his throat. "My business is urgent. Haste is of great importance. Could I not go with the messenger myself?"

"Oswald has been in exile among us for nearly twenty years." The old woman clasped her hands across her worn gown. "No business requires such haste that we ought to relax caution. You will go with these men. They will keep you under watch until we hear if the prince will see you." She nodded toward the door. Luthwin saw two Scots waiting for them.

The guards put the three travelers in another beehive house and closed the door. For the first time since they left the raiding party, Reud quit watching them.

He knows we cannot get away any more than he can, Luthwin thought.

The Briton pulled a tin canteen from his tunic and took a long drink. Through the smoke hole in the top of the hut Luthwin watched the daylight fade. In the darkness he could hear Reud drinking from his canteen again. He moved closer to Wallen. When Reud began to snore, he put his hand on his friend's arm. "What do you suppose he is doing here?" he whispered. "Oswald is a brother of Eanfrid, the heir to Bernicia's crown."

"Then why is he in exile?" Wallen's arm stiffened.

"It is some enmity between the house of Bernicia and the house of Deira." Luthwin couldn't keep the excitement out of his voice. "Edwin was strong enough to rule both provinces and unite the Northumbrians. Eanfrid was too young to hold his territory. So he fled. I have heard my father speak of it many times. Do you suppose Reud will—" The snoring stopped. Reud turned over. In his sleep he mumbled something. Wallen leaned his head nearer to Luthwin. "Do you suppose he has come to get Oswald to go back and lead the Northumbrians?"

That is what I wondered. Luthwin leaned back on the hard floor. But why would Reud bring a leader for the Saxons? He had been with the Briton raiders just days before. Luthwin fell asleep with the question puzzling him.

The two Scots opened the door before daybreak. By torchlight they led them to a long stone building on the shore. On a bench inside sat the prince. With him stood two men wearing white robes much like the ones the bishop and Deacon James wore at the royal villa.

"Please sit down," Oswald said. He waited until they sat facing him. The prince saw no one but Reud. Luthwin had time to notice every detail of his appearance. "Then you are Reud, the slave from my father's house?" A smile softened the prince's stern expression.

"Yes, my lord." Reud pulled his shoulders straight.

Oswald seemed to expect him to explain something. To Luthwin's surprise the big Briton appeared unnerved.

"I am that same Briton, my lord. I have come on very personal business. Would it be possible—"

The prince shook his head. "It is not possible. Speak your mind, my friend. You need hide nothing from these good men. They hear a great deal, and never does a word of it go beyond the walls of confidence."

"But the lads—" Reud began.

"Why, they are with you, are they not? Come now. Let us not waste the time you felt was so precious. I rowed all night in a coracle with these brothers to come from Iona."

Reud clenched his hands together, his whole frame trembling. "Then let me be first, my lord, to invite you to return to your native land!" He drew a deep breath. "Edwin is dead. With my own sword I fought in the battle, and I saw him fall. Even now his kingdom has fallen apart. The Mercians and the Britons unite, and the two have laid waste all of Deira. I fought with my own people, but I struggled only to bring the rightful prince back to his own!" He slumped on the bench, tears coursing down his cheeks.

"You forget that I am my father's younger son." Oswald rose. He stood a moment looking at the Briton, then dropped to his knees before him. "But, old friend, you have brought me greater riches than the kingdom!" His voice broke. "I have longed to see you since the day I left home. I thought you must surely be dead, or you would have found me in my exile."

Reud raised his head. "I could not come without doing something first to give you back what was yours." He stood and lifted Oswald to his feet, looking humble now, and yet strangely proud, Luthwin thought. "I have secret agreements with thanes and eorls all up the coast, and even many Britons your father treated with kindness have promised friendship. If you should return, they would rally around you."

Oswald smiled, then turned away. "Who are these lads, then?"

The Briton was speechless. In his fervor he had apparently forgotten them. Now his face worked in confusion as he tried to find something to say.

Luthwin bowed before Oswald. "I am the son of Hunwold, my lord. He is an eorl of the Pictish border. Perhaps you know—"

"Hunwold fought side by side with Edwin!" Reud interrupted, suddenly excited. "He would have no agreement with your party as long as Edwin lived and reigned."

"And when his king was dead?"

Reud glanced at Luthwin, then back at the prince. "My lord, I did not speak with him after the battle. It was a complete victory for the Britons—a great slaughter."

"Does Hunwold live, then?" Oswald asked.

"I do not know, my lord."

"Then the lads are your captives?"

"Yes, my lord. When I found out who they were."

Oswald sighed. "I have much to tell you, Reud. I have learned much in my exile. One of the things I have learned is that men are brothers, of whatever rank their birth. And indeed, you and I knew that from boyhood, or you would not be here. We must return the lads to Hunwold."

"But Hunwold did nothing to repress Edwin when you and your brother were young and could not defend your kingdom."

"We must forgive, Reud. Have you forgotten so soon the religion you professed in our youth?"

Reud bowed his head. "I have not forgotten, but I have ceased to have faith. A man must work out what he can from life. I have forgiven too many already. Some men are without honor and do not deserve forgiveness."

"No, my friend, you are wrong. We do not deserve God's forgiveness, yet He forgives us." Oswald paced the room, thinking.

Luthwin watched the prince's face. The man was a strange prince. None of the usual lines of determination crossed his jaw. His eyes betrayed no love of power or wish for revenge.

"If what you say is true," Oswald said, "and not just the fond wishes of a faithful friend, I must return to my countrymen. They have had the ravages of war for generations, though. I suppose it is a part of the Saxon character. But even that is not beyond the reach of the power of Christ. I will go!"

As quickly as he had spoken the word, he began to act. He sent messengers to Northumbria, and Reud went with them, the most trusted ambassador the prince knew. Another messenger went to Hunwold. Oswald would not allow Luthwin to travel during the hazardous winter storms. "I will take you when I go myself, when matters are settled in the spring," he promised.

By coracle the boys traveled with him to Iona. He settled them in a hut under the care of a deacon at the island mission. "You are to spend the winter in study," he told them.

When Wallen objected that he was but a servant, Oswald laughed. "But all of the teachers here are of your Celtic race. How will your young master learn unless you help him understand their language?"

Like the brothers in the school, Luthwin and Wallen wore the white woolen tunics that reached to their feet. Daily they studied Latin. But most of each day they spent with Aiden.

The Irish teacher sat with them for hours at a time, telling them stories, the Sacred Word open on his knees, something the youths considered much better than having to struggle over strange words and script. Even in Wallen's slow translations, the stories were more interesting than the long battle epics the thanes told in Hunwold's hall.

"How different Aiden is from Bishop Paulinus!" Luthwin once exclaimed to Wallen.

The older boy grinned. "He certainly has no haughty manners or rich clothing. If he were my only teacher, I think I would like to go to school."

"But his teachings are different, too," Luthwin said. "He keeps a different holy day. His way is gentle. He does not grow angry and give ugly warnings."

Together the two boys taught Aiden the Saxon language. "Someday I will come as a missionary to your land," he assured them. "This is my calling from God. I will be ready when the time comes for me to leave Iona."

Chapter Five

THE SMALL peat fire warmed only the center of the beehive hut. Luthwin drew his robe's hood close around his ears and blew out his breath in three puffs of white. "I wish these houses were as warm as the brothers' hearts," he remarked, shivering. It was time for them to study the Scriptures, but he wondered how much he could learn while he was so cold.

"The winter will soon be over," Wallen reminded him. "And then we will go home." He stretched his arms above the red embers and grinned. "I think my mother is a better cook than Brother Finnel. I am growing tired of oat porridge."

"Me, too!" Luthwin's mouth watered from just thinking about Ceda's cakes topped with plenty of honey and nuts.

The door rattled. Someone on the outside was trying to work the ice from the latch. Luthwin jumped up and hit the door firmly twice, then pulled it open.

"Welcome!" He laughed. "Brother Aiden, you are made entirely of snow, with your beard frosted over, too. Come, warm yourself by our fire."

The teacher sat beside Wallen on his bench and stuck his feet from under his robe. Luthwin gasped. The man's feet were bare, and tough and red from walking in the snow.

"Brother Aiden, where are your shoes?" Luthwin blurted without thinking.

Embarrassed, Aiden replied, "A young peasant joined our school yesterday. He had no shoes, and he was just a slight lad. I am used to the cold."

"Are there not more sheepskins in the storehouse?" Luthwin asked.

Aiden smiled. "Ah, yes, but I have no time to be stitching shoes for myself."

Luthwin looked at his friend, who nodded. "We could make you some warm sheepskin leggings like the Saxons wear."

Aiden drew his white robe around his ankles and took out his parchment scroll. "In this school we do not ask pay for teachers, but I would gladly accept such a loving gift."

That day when the brother recited the story of the Good Shepherd, Luthwin thought of how much Aiden was like Christ. This is what being a Christian ought to mean, he thought. I could accept such teaching if it makes a person as good as Aiden. And not once had Aiden ever mentioned the burning of people the bishop kept talking about.

Something inside him stirred Luthwin. When the Scriptures lay on the table before him, he yearned to understand the words written there. But even now, after weeks of study, he could understand only a few Latin words. The marks on parchment remained as empty of meaning as the ancient runes Sigbert used for his magic.

For two months ice chunks floating with the current filled the channel between Iona and the shore. At last a warm breeze cleared the water. Tiny green sprigs showed through the snow and stones around the beehive houses on the island, and Luthwin waited impatiently for Oswald to send for him and Wallen.

Now on warm afternoons they often studied in the sunlight. They also watched the brothers copying in the scriptorium and marveled at the beauty of the small scrolls they made of colored parchment lettered with bright inks of red and gold and blue.

One bright morning Luthwin sat with Wallen on the rocks along the water, watching the seabirds soaring and diving. Brother Aiden came so softly that they did not hear him until he sat down beside them.

"This is a blessed day," he mused aloud. "Spring and the Sabbath work together to give us double joys."

Luthwin turned to look at Aiden. "Why is it that here we worship on a day different from the day the Christians at Edwin's villa worshiped?" he asked. He had wondered for many weeks why Aiden and the other teachers did not keep the first day of the week sacred, as did Bishop Paulinus.

"They think they do right to follow the customs of the teachers from Rome," Aiden replied. "But we find no instruction in the Word of God to forsake the day He gave His blessing to when He made our world. Our Lord worshiped the Father on this day. We would live as He lived, Luthwin."

Aiden scanned the water and the distant shores of the larger island of England. "The Sabbath is a remembrance of God's great work to make our earth. Is it not a fitting day to spend in meditation under the sky?"

Luthwin thought of the time Bishop Paulinus visited his father's ton. Ceda had said then that the Christian God was the One who had made the world. Yes, the youth decided, He was worthy of worship if He could do that.

The next day a deacon came to their hut. "Lads, we must send you to Oswald now," he said. "You have been a blessing to us all. God bless you and return you safely to your father's house."

Unexpected feelings came over Luthwin. When he took off the white woolen robe, he felt strange wearing ordinary Saxon clothes.

"You do not fit into these leggings as you did when I found them for you." Wallen chuckled. "Luthwin, you have grown like a spring dandelion!"

The Saxon youth tried to loosen the sleeves of his shirt. They bound his arms tight almost to his elbows now. "It must be the oat porridge." He laughed, but he did not worry about how his clothes looked. He was going home!

Oswald's party entered the Tweed Valley in two days. Marching swiftly, they reached Hunwold's Mark at the end of the week. Luthwin felt strange standing there so near home, waiting for an answer to the blast of the horn.

Hunwold wanted to show his thanks to the prince for bringing Luthwin home, especially since Raedfrith, Luthwin's older brother, had died in battle; but Oswald would not accept the Saxon leader's hospitality.

"There will be years ahead for me to feast at your table, friend," he said. "But there may be only weeks to gather all the Humbrenes together against the enemies. I must rally our forces and help my brother get ready for the long conflict."

Hunwold lay his sword across his knees. "I have word that your brother has already strengthened his forces near the Wall. But you are right. You must do all you can to help him. And when you call on me, I will be with you," he promised. "My spear is always ready to defend this kingdom, my lord."

Oswald smiled grimly. "May the good God bless your hands with success. You will serve the kingdom best right now by maintaining your strength here against an invasion from the north or the west."

After the prince left, Luthwin spent hours with his father. The old eorl sat in his great hall talking seriously with his thanes or planning tactics for future defenses. His face seemed more deeply lined than when Luthwin left. He hardly laughed, even when they feasted and mead ran heavy.

He is still grieving for Raedfrith, Luthwin thought. His brother had been too young for battle, some of the men said, but he had fought bravely.

"Raedfrith carried Edwin's banner until the enemy struck him down," Hunwold told him, his voice a mixture of sadness and pride. "He did not dishonor his people by fleeing in the heat of battle even though he was but a youth."

During the late autumn while Hunwold was in the south with Edwin, the Picts had crossed the borders, raiding the farms of the eorls nearby. Luthwin stared at the new collection of shields and spears his father had taken in reprisal when he returned.

"These are what we have left after I gave rich booty to the thanes who went with me," Hunwold said. "But if we have a long struggle driving out the followers of Cadwallon and Penda, we will need all the defense we can get."

"Do you think Eanfrid and Oswald will be able to unite the Humbrenes?" Luthwin thought of Edwin's son, safe now with his uncle in Kent. "Father, why did you not support Eanfrid when he fled before? He was the rightful prince."

The old eorl shook his head. "Luthwin, he was but a lad. And it takes a strong and experienced man to hold a kingdom together and defend it in times of stress. Edwin was already uniting the southern province. Mercia and even the West Saxons acknowledged him as their overlord. I could see that under his strong leadership our country would be as strong as he was."

"Then someday Edwin's son may come back to his kingdom if he is worthy of it?"

"Yes, my son. If he is worthy of the responsibility. Among the Saxons a prince does not rule just because his father was king, but because he is wise and strong in battle. There will always be princes, but few of them are worthy."

Luthwin wondered what kind of leader Oswald's brother would be. Certainly Oswald resembled no Saxon hero he had ever heard about. Try as he would, Luthwin could not imagine him enraged with the excitement of battle glory, waving an ax and screaming as he rode to fight.

Summer was lonely for Luthwin. When he rode Twi around the ton, he rode alone. Wallen worked in the fields, plowing and planting. Fourteen now, the slave youth toiled with the men.

"It is not right that you should be a slave!" Luthwin often protested.

Wallen only laughed. "I am as strong as many seasoned workers already," he boasted. "I can lift the full bags with no help. And that is more than Brum can do, though he is taller and heavier than I am."

Luthwin knew about the rivalry between his friend and the son of his father's most troublesome slave. Brum always complained because Wallen got special favors, and he was as eager to fight as the young cocks in the barnyard.

The passing summer days saw the whole ton stirring with unrest. The ceorls came from their farms more often than usual. Women and children who should have tended the gardens outside the ton spent hours working in the sheds inside the wall, as if afraid to be without protection. Luthwin could not remember a time like it on the Tweed.

He listened intently to every word he heard about the coming struggle. Eanfrid was busy knitting the Bernicians together strongly enough to withstand Cadwallon, who now held York and sent his British army on savage expeditions deep into the northern province to destroy the countryside.

Luthwin realized it was only a matter of weeks before the terrible struggle reached the northern border. Hunwold had defeated the Scots and Picts, but Luthwin knew that even his father could not also drive off the Britons if they all attacked at once. Each time he looked around the ton, he remembered the ruins where he and Wallen had once found shelter. Secretly he practiced with his sword on horseback and on foot, for if an enemy came, he would stand beside his father to defend the estate. He could not bear to live through the coming years, if he should survive, to see the wreckage or lose his family.

One afternoon in the great hall, Hunwold rose from his council seat. "Luthwin, come with me," he said. He led his son through the long passage on the north side of the bower. Luthwin watched silently while he opened a heavy door, entering one of the storage chambers. He moved two wooden boxes, then pulled out a leather and ivory chest.

Lifting its cover, he turned to his son and said, "These are times of unrest. Since I may not live until you are the age to receive this sword with proper ceremony, I must give it to you myself."

Luthwin watched his father unwrap an ancient weapon, its bent and dulled blade showing patches of rust. "It is very old, Father."

"Indeed!" Hunwold straightened and looked at Luthwin. "My son, it is a gift from your noble ancestors. Since you are now my only son—" His voice trembled with emotion, but he cleared his throat and went on. "This sword in your hands will make you a great leader if you have the heart of a leader. Look at me, Luthwin. I see in your face the strength of an eorl, a prince. Be worthy of the gifts you have inherited. Bear yourself proudly always, for you are the offspring of Woden himself."

Luthwin's fingers clutched the hilt of the old sword. His heart thrilled at his father s words. "Where shall I keep it?" he asked.

"I do not wish to know," Hunwold answered. "The owner of such a gift must possess great wisdom. You must now use understanding and be a man to make decisions."

All at once Luthwin felt like laughing. But he must not. So now by some magic in the sword he was wise. He thought of all the hours he had spent trying to learn to read. And still he could understand only a few words, a few marks. "I will care for it to honor your trust," he said seriously.

Hunwold nodded. He closed the chest, pushed the other boxes in front of it again, and they locked the door to the storeroom. His father said nothing about its being a secret, but Luthwin understood that no one must see the sword in public. He tucked it under his tunic and slipped to his own chamber.

But though the sword remained a secret from everyone else, Luthwin would not keep it from Wallen. When the cookshed was empty that evening, he brought his friend there. "We will sharpen this sword and hide it," he said, flashing the blade in the firelight.

Together they polished it, smoothed its hilt, and made its edge keen again. When they finished several days later, Wallen brought the wooden scabbard he had found at the ruined ton.

"It fits." Luthwin sighed. "Now you must hide it for me, Wallen. Someday soon we will have a battle here. I have my new sword. You also must be armed!"

Wallen raised his eyebrows. "A slave is not allowed to possess arms," he objected. "If I were found out—"

"Just hide it where it will keep safe and dry."

Wallen grinned, patting the scabbard inside his short tunic. "I will not use it until you say so." News of raids came daily.

"We must post double watch day and night," Hunwold warned the men in the great hall one evening. "I will call all the coerls to duty. What must be finished in the fields, the slaves can do."

That night sleeping thanes crowded the great hall. In the sheds which housed the food during the winter, the coerls settled their wives and children. Ladies from smaller tons moved into the chambers where Luthwin's mother lived. The quiet settlement had become a fortress.

In the morning Luthwin found Wallen before he went to the fields. They slipped into Ceda's wattle hut. "You must bring in the sword today." He knew his voice quivered with the excitement he felt. "Keep it with you while you work from now on. You can hide it under your tunic. Wallen, if the enemy comes, you must not be without a way to defend yourself."

"But what if Eldred finds me with it—or the slave overseer?" Wallen's face blanched. "A slave can be killed for just having a knife. It would look as if I were a traitor getting ready to join the enemy." They walked around the stable to harness old Thundor for work.

Luthwin tried to feel the confidence he forced into his voice. "I will talk with Eldred if I need to. If the danger were not great, my father would not call the countryfolk in."

"I will bring the sword tonight," the Celtic slave said, tightening his belt over his loose tunic. He cracked his whip over Thundor's brindled back, and the ox moved out through the gate with awkward, hurried steps.

"Your mother wishes to see you in her quarters," Ceda said, coming from the larder with a basket of meal. Luthwin ran to the bower, his mind busy with what might happen today.

"Excuse me, madam." He felt his cheeks redden. He had nearly stepped on the train of a lady's gown. He dodged children playing with tiny wooden dolls on the stone floor of the hallway, then stopped suddenly at the door of his mother's chamber to catch his breath.

"Luthwin!" his mother called. "Come in, my son. I must talk with you."

Luthwin bowed to her and sat down on the bench beside her. He noticed she had been crying. Suddenly he felt awkward. "Yes, Mother?"

"My son, I have lost your two brothers in battle—Theobald in the fight with the Picts three years past, and Raedfrith with Edwin at Heathfield." She stopped, her eyes searching Luthwin's until he could hardly control the surge of emotion rising inside him.

Squeezing her hand, Luthwin knew what she would ask of him. He could think of nothing to say.

"I thought I had lost you too when we heard that the Britons had destroyed the royal villa. But some miracle of the gods gave you back to me. I cannot bear to lose you, my last child!"

"But, Mother—"

Her fingers gripped his until they felt cold; her eyes were bright with a fear that jumped the space between them and settled over his heart like a warrior's death shroud.

"But I must help my father defend our home. I am a Saxon!"

His mother nodded, her eyes releasing him for a moment. "And your creed is to serve honorably or die defending." She tried so hard to smile that it almost tempted Luthwin to relent.

"But I am nearly thirteen years old," he reminded himself. "I am almost as tall as many of the thanes. If I love mother, I must help to take care of her."

She dropped his hand and folded hers in her lap, resolution firming her mouth to a stiff line. "A Saxon woman knows how to die with honor, too. Go, my son. Your father may need you, as you say. And I must be of help to the ladies who are my guests."

She removed the needlework from her lap. Seconds later Luthwin listened to the jingle of the keys dangling from her belt as she walked down the hallway and out into the courtyard.

He walked the same hallway, his steps lagging. All morning he fought the dread building up inside him, overshadowing every thought. Sitting on the end bench in the great hall, he half listened to the reports of the messenger sent to tell them of encounters with Britons all down the coast. The man's singsong voice recited numbers and places meaningless to Luthwin. What had they to do with the danger that threatened to blot out Hunwold's ton? The bold deeds he recited were nothing. Bernicia was nothing. Home was everything today.

I am not behaving like a Saxon! Luthwin suddenly scolded himself, pulling his thoughts together and forcing his ears to listen.

The messenger waved his sword, his voice sharp with challenge. "No man of Saxon blood is safe in this land!" he shouted. "Cadwallon has vowed he will extinguish our race and return the whole island to his own people. It will be Britannia again, and not England. He swears not a Saxon will remain to breathe this air or till this soil."

A rumble of voices echoed through the room. Luthwin glanced from face to face. The thanes were ready, their chins grimly set, their eyes fierce. He knew they believed the messenger. Had they not seen the wreckage of Cadwallon's warfare for themselves?

Hunwold stood beside his carved seat. "We have not fallen!" His voice rang with pride through the timbers of the hall to its ceiling. "I have seen this Briton on the battlefield. Truly he is like a beast in his passion to tear and to destroy. And he would certainly do as he threatens if he could defeat us. But he too is a man. He too may die by the sword. I am an old man, but I have not laid down my spear. While I have breath, I shall not lay it down."

"Aye!" Every man in the hall rose to his feet, shouting. Luthwin joined them.

When the room quieted, Luthwin looked around, embarrassed. "Where has Cadwallon struck this time?" he whispered to the thane sitting nearest him.

"What? Are you a stone that you did not hear?" The thane rubbed his hands down his knees and stared at him. "He did not speak of raids. He spoke of murder!"

Luthwin eased himself back to the bench, his knees shaking.

"Eanfrid has been murdered in Cadwallon's house, where he went to plead for the peace of our land. The Briton claims he will offer no mercy!"

"Where is Oswald? Did he dare to enter Cadwallon's territory, too?"

The thane laughed, a bitter smile curving his mouth. "Is there anywhere in all Northumbria that can boast it is free from the Briton demon?"

"What he does not control, Penda does!" Eldred, Hunwold's chief thane, stopped in front of Luthwin. "The two of them are like wolves gone mad. They think of nothing but what they will devour next."

"We cannot sit idly within our walls waiting for the beasts to fall upon us!" someone shouted. The room quieted. "Where is Sigbert? Let him cast a spell on our enemies, for they are divided in their religion. Maybe our gods will come to our aid as with the ancient heroes."

"Aye!" The shout rang with conviction.

Sigbert came from the corner of the hall and stood opposite Hunwold. "Then bring me the oldest sword in your possession, and I will write on it the magic runes that will bring us victory!" He lifted his arms high and began to chant words Luthwin could not understand.

"He speaks the language of our fathers before it became corrupted by mixture with other tongues," Eldred explained. "It is the language which Woden hears, so Sigbert says."

With his spear, the priest marked the floor, screaming louder and still louder. Suddenly he stood still. "And now bring me the sword," he said. "It must be the oldest sword among us." He closed his eyes and rocked to and fro on his heels. Luthwin waited, his breath caught on the lump in his throat.

"I can see the weapon. It is one used by Hunwold's grandfather in many battles. I see it covered with rust and bent by many blows against byrnies and shields. On its bronze hilt I will draw powerful runes. On its blade of iron I will write words that will turn our enemies to cowards."

Sigbert opened his eyes. With great dignity he returned to his bench along the wall. Everyone turned to Hunwold.

Luthwin wondered if his father believed in Sigbert's power. But why do I question it? the youth asked himself. Have I not always believed? He slipped through the crowded room to his father. Hunwold held out his hand for him to wait.

"I will send for the sword."

Luthwin leaned forward. "If you give me permission, I will bring it."

"Yes, my son, bring it quickly, for the men are anxious." Luthwin dashed to the stable and mounted Twi without a saddle.

"I am forbidden to open the gate," the watchman objected.

Now Luthwin had no time for quibbling. "My father has just ordered it," Luthwin shouted, his voice ringing with an authority that sounded strange to his own ears. He grasped the oak bar that held the gate in place. Reluctantly the gateman helped him.

Again he jumped on Twi and raced down the hillside to the new field where Wallen plowed today. The slave saw him coming and stopped plowing.

"I must have the sword now!" Luthwin gasped, breathless.

Wallen threw him the rope with which he led the ox. "Then you hold Thundor while I'm gone. It will not take long."

He dashed across the field and disappeared into the bushes. Up the rocky slope Luthwin saw bushes move, indicating his friend's progress. In minutes Wallen came out again. Luthwin thought he could not possibly be carrying a sword because of the way he ran. Had he forgotten where he put it?

The Celt stopped beside Thundor, his face pale. "The sword is gone!" he whispered. "I put it carefully under some small rocks on the ledge in an overhang. But someone has taken it."

Luthwin gripped his shoulder. Neither had shared the secret with anyone else. Had someone followed Wallen when he hid it?

Luthwin choked, thinking of the men waiting in the great hall.

"My father must have it! Sigbert is going to write magic runes on its blade. My father's grandfather used it when he conquered this land."

Wallen shivered. Luthwin felt his own shoulder muscles tighten. "What will you tell Hunwold?" the slave asked.

Luthwin met his friend's eyes. "I will take the responsibility myself.

The sword is mine, and he told me to make the decision of where to keep it."

Returning through the woods, he took the long way back to the ton, trying to think of an explanation. The gateman opened the gate when he called. Luthwin did not care that he muttered under his breath.

When he entered the great hall, a hush surrounded him. With everyone watching him, he walked to his father's seat. He bowed his head and whispered so that no one else could hear.

"The sword is stolen."

Hunwold did not move. "Are you certain?" he asked, keeping his voice as low as his son's. "Are you sure you did not take it out and put it somewhere else later?"

"I am sure." Luthwin felt his father's eyes drilling into him. "I repaired the sword and polished off the rust. I took it to the rocks along the bluff and hid it under a ledge. Now it is gone."

"Did someone see you?"

"I do not know."

"I alone am responsible," Hunwold said, his voice still barely audible. "You are too young. Go to your mother, Luthwin."

Luthwin trembled. His face burned, but he dared not beg pardon here. His father stood up. The youth backed away and ran from the hall. Not since he received his gifts on his twelfth birthday had his father sent him in such a manner to his mother.

He did not need to tell her why he came. She guessed from his face. He was grateful at least that she asked nothing. All day he ran errands for her as he used to when he was too young to enter the great hall councils to listen to the men's talk. If only he could avoid the eyes of the ladies in the hallways and the bower and the storerooms! On their faces he could read their thoughts. They knew that he had fallen into disgrace in some way.

Across the courtyard he heard the uproar in the great hall. It was nearly time for the evening meal. Luthwin waited for a chance to slip away from the women's quarters. He had to know what was happening.

When it turned dark enough, he stole to the end of the great hall. Wedging his toes between the timbers, he climbed as high as the sloped roof. At its end a supporting beam stuck out. Luthwin perched on it and pulled back the thatching so that he could see inside.

Hunwold sat in his carved seat, leaning forward while an eorl from a nearby ton addressed the assembly. His voice rose and fell, and Luthwin strained to hear. The man spoke of devotion to Woden and kept appealing to Sigbert to uphold what he said. Finally he sat down.

A lesser eorl from the coast asked permission to speak. Hunwold nodded. Walking to the raised floor where Hunwold sat, the eorl faced the men. "I say that Woden is left behind us!" His shout echoed through the dark rafters. A murmur passed over the group. "I say our ancestors left Woden behind when they came to this island. He has not helped us or our fathers before us. Those who have forsaken Woden grow strong, while those who serve him most faithfully are the puppets of greater lords."

Luthwin saw many thanes nodding in agreement. Sigbert started to rise, but sat back down.

The eorl went on in a louder, clearer voice: "Edwin was not a follower of Woden when he reached his greatest power. He overthrew the house of Bernicia and sent his emissaries even across the seas. He subdued Mercia and all the lands to the south until he ruled as the king of all the English."

"Aye, but he fell by the sword!" Sigbert interrupted.

"Such is the lot of all men!" The eorl pointed a steady finger at the priest of Woden. "You too will die in your appointed time."

He turned to address Hunwold. "My lord, it is foolishness to put our trust in superstitions passed on to us from ancient times. Our fathers were brave and great warriors, but they were also mortal. And if Woden was our ancestor, as many of us claim, he, too, was a mortal and is now dead."

Hunwold held up his hands for silence. "My fellow Saxons, you all know that I journeyed to Edwin's court nearly a year ago to speak of this matter with the king. I was not convinced, as the king believed, that the way of Christ is the way of life. But I am also in doubt about the spells and magic to which we have given our trust in the past. They have not helped us."

Eldred spoke from where he had stood during the entire council. Luthwin turned on his perch to see better.

"I have lived long and have seen many lords and great men," the old thane said. "I have seen famines and plenty, success and defeat. And the warriors faithful to Woden presented him with favors, sacrificing their goods and their food to him. They sacrificed in good years and bad. And a fate stronger than Woden moved the seasons with a power that no magic could change."

The old man reached for a table to support himself. His gray hair gleamed in the torchlight. "A man is subject to a power beyond what we understand, above and beyond Woden and Thor or the other spirits that frightened me in my youth. I do not know what god this power is, but let us be up to the fight like men and make our own fortunes and cease arguing to no good about childish fears. Our defense lies in our own hands. Are we so weak that we must seek the help of runes and mysterious markings instead of our strength?" His voice wavered, and he sat down, wiping the sweat from his face.

Luthwin considered what he had heard for a moment. The sudden flare of a torch in the courtyard below startled him.

"A slave has escaped!" Luthwin recognized the voice of the overseer. "A youth from among the field hands is gone! Brum. You know the one, Hunwold!"

"He has gone to inform the enemy!" a thane shouted as the men took up their spears.

Chapter Six

LUTHWIN SCRAMBLED down the logs on the end of the great hall. Behind the sheds he dashed to the cookshed. "Ceda, where is Wallen?" he gasped.

"All the men and boys from the fields are in the stable," she answered. "The lords are already questioning them." Ceda stopped stirring the broth long enough to stack barley loaves high on a tin tray.

Luthwin noticed the worried look haunting her eyes.

"I fear the Saxons will trust none of us now," she said. "Your father will wonder if all of his slaves will rush at the first chance to aid the enemy."

"That is not so," Luthwin objected. "My father knows his servants—each one." He paused and bit his lip. "But if I were a slave—"

An outcry from the stables sent him running there before he finished his sentence. The overseer held his whip high over the back of Brum's father. With all the strength of his bulging muscles, he brought it down again and again. The slave gritted his teeth. Luthwin turned his head. Even Brum's father, who made so much trouble for everyone, did not deserve such a beating.

The overseer laid the whip down and pulled the Briton around to face him. "You are responsible for your son!" he shouted, shaking the trembling man. "If you had been loyal, he would have stayed in Hunwold's service. You shall pay from your food allotment until you have paid the price he would bring in markets across the channel." His voice dropped off in a snarling hiss.

"Why, that family will starve!" someone dared whisper. "Already they have been under penalty for the pig the old man stole last winter."

"It is just," another voice answered. "A man must pay for his crimes."

Luthwin looked back to the overseer, who glared at the Britons lined up before him. "Each of you is to see that his own children are about their duties," the Saxon said. "If anyone else runs away, the nearest of kin will pay with his life."

The Celts stood stony-faced. Luthwin did not immediately see Wallen, and searched to meet his friends eyes. Wallen looked straight ahead, seemingly unconcerned.

"The overseer is foolish to let the first one off alive," a thane commented. "I would make an example of the old thief. He would be a small loss to Hunwold." A murmur of agreement followed.

The Saxons broke into small groups and moved back toward the courtyard. One warrior brandished his sword as if he meant to kill every Celt on the estate at once. "And I say, if we are attacked, we ought to get them before they turn to the enemy. This may be Hunwold's ton, but all of us depend on it for shelter. We cannot afford to risk our lives for slaves!"

Luthwin shuddered. Somehow he must warn his friend. But with the thanes feeling the way they did, he did not dare speak openly. He waited until the company in the great hall slept. Because of his disgrace in the morning, he must sleep in the women's quarters with the smaller boys tonight. In the crowded space no one would miss him.

He whispered at the door of Ceda's hut. A hand pulled back the hide covering the doorway, and he slipped inside and sat down beside Wallen on the straw. "I heard the men talking after the whipping," Luthwin said. "I am afraid for both of you."

"But we have been faithful in our work, and Hunwold knows it, as you said before," Ceda interrupted. "We have had nothing to do with the bands of free Celts living in the hills. Not since my husband died."

"But someone is sure to remember that he was not a slave," Luthwin said. "And the thanes are afraid." How could he explain the furor that stirred the men in the ton tonight?

Wallen chuckled softly, his voice rich with scorn. "A Saxon afraid? Battle gives a Saxon more pleasure than even a feast does! The men do nothing for entertainment but sing of their battle adventures."

"That is true." Luthwin clenched his knuckles and leaned forward. "But it is different to meet an enemy on the battlefield. Here a vast army may surround us. The men talk wildly about being burned out. They fear the Celts on the inside might help their kinsmen get inside the gates. I heard one man say you must all be killed if we are attacked."

Ceda drew in her breath. "Hunwold is just. He would never allow that. He knows those he can trust. You said so yourself, Luthwin."

"An eorl is a leader, and no more," Luthwin reminded her, "Even the youngest thane is free to disagree with my father. And strangers have come here for protection. They may cast their voices against Hunwold's command."

"But what could we do to protect ourselves?" Wallen's voice sounded more serious than usual.

"You can escape."

"We cannot flee." Wallen spoke slowly, deliberately. "You know what the overseer warned. Besides, it would seem to be proof that we side with Cadwallon. And we could never come back."

"Surely you could find some way for both of you to leave. You would be free!" Luthwin's heart beat rapidly at the idea.

"Running away does not make one free." Wallen stood up and pulled back the covering from the doorway.

"I want you to stay alive," Luthwin said. He stepped outside and darted through the shadows toward the bowers and his bed. His heart ached.

In the morning the overseer put men to work in the field just beyond the enclosure, allowing only one from each family outside the wall. "We will take no chances," he told Hunwold. "If they know the penalty, they will not leave."

Hunwold's mouth was stern. "I want no slave killing. Bring any offender to me. Do you understand?"

The overseer shrugged. Luthwin thought he seemed eager to carry out his threat against the Celts.

With Hunwold, Luthwin walked through the ton. His father inspected the wooden ramparts again. He seemed satisfied with what he found, and said nothing about the lost sword.

"I have instructed each ceorl to make himself a wooden spear," he told Eldred when they stopped before the great hall. "Each youth strong enough to thrust a fork in the fields is old enough to be armed to defend the ton."

The aged thane nodded his approval. "And your own son should stand by your side. Blood binds you together. He is a brave lad, Hunwold."

Luthwin tried to meet his father's eyes. Would Hunwold forgive him for losing the sword? he wondered.

"Yes, my son will carry his own sword and defend our ton."

It was not yet midday when a watchman Hunwold had stationed on a hillside in the forest galloped into the ton. The throng of men in the courtyard hushed as he jumped from his horse and ran to the hall. Luthwin dashed inside close behind him.

"I have seen movements on the Pictish side of the river," the man panted. "And upstream a line of horses is coining through a narrow gorge from the south."

At once guards brought the slaves from the field. The overseer counted them at the gate and barred it. Now it would open for no one. The gateman climbed the ladder to watch from his tower.

"Where is your sword, Luthwin?" Eldred demanded. "Behave yourself bravely today, and Saxons will sing of your youthful valor for a hundred years." The old man smiled reassurance.

Luthwin touched his hand to the place where his sword should hang. He had left it in his chamber.

Hunwold glanced at him and frowned. "Always be prepared, my son," he said. He walked to the middle of the courtyard and raised his arms for silence. The crowd turned to listen to his command. "If the Britons meet us in open battle, we will stand, each man as I have given him his position. Spearmen and axmen first to the center, with three ranks in a solid shield wall."

"And if darkness comes before they attack, what shall we do?" a voice challenged. "Shall we burn alive when they set the ton afire?"

Hunwold searched out the speaker in the crowd. "Is your heart so weak that you face battle with panic?" His voice boomed. "We will preserve both our lives and this place. Remain ready. That is your duty."

The armed men around him fixed their eyes on the watchman. Luthwin brought his sword and also watched. To him the afternoon seemed longer than a month. The sun moved like a wounded man, slowly, very slowly, across the sky.

The Britons did not attack. Night came finally, and with the darkness, Hunwold gave his command. Everyone within the barricade must pull thatching from the buildings within reach of the wall. After they heaped the dry stuff in the courtyard, someone struck a flame to it. The blaze roared, the heat driving back those who carried more armfuls of straw from the smaller sheds.

"It is better to have the fire here in the center to give light to protect us from night attack than to have the enemy set the whole ton aflame," a woman explained. Luthwin recognized his mothers voice. Red-faced from the heat, she worked with the wives of ceorls and thanes. Across the courtyard he saw the bare rafters of her bower outlined in the firelight.

"Straw will not burn all night!" someone shouted. "What of our safety when the straw has burned?"

A thane from another ton waved his arms, shouting, "To the huts! Let us burn the slave huts. They are partly wood. That will burn for hours."

A rush to the end of the ton answered his cry. Men dragged the flimsy pole and wattle shelters to the ground. In the space where they used to stand, the men heaped the materials from the huts together. Fire swept up the pile, crackling, making a pillar of smoke that swirled with bits of burning twigs.

Luthwin found Wallen standing in the shadow of the stable. "I think you ought to go over the wall," he warned. "You can see how wild they are with the excitement of danger. And any minute they might turn with their weapons on the slaves."

Wallen shook his head. "I could not do that. What would I do on the outside if you and your family are inside? And I would not belong with the Britons battering the outside of the ton. I will stay here. I may yet be able to help."

"But how?" Luthwin glanced around them. No one apparently noticed him talking with the slave boy.

"You say your father trusts me. If you really believe he does, take me to him now. I think I can do something no one else will do tonight."

Luthwin shook his head. A dull throbbing began between his ears. Breathing smoke had made his throat sore. "But, Wallen," he began.

His friend said nothing.

"I will find him, then. We will meet you in the smith's shop if he can get away from his men."

Hunwold stood at the end of the courtyard, ready to give further orders. He listened, but Luthwin sensed his impatience. "What can a boy do that would help?" he objected. "Yes, I trust him. Already he has proved his worth when he stayed with you through the journey from Edwin's villa."

"Just listen to what he wants to tell you," Luthwin pleaded.

In the smith's shop an hour later, Wallen called to them in a whisper. Luthwin saw him in a corner beside the forge.

"Tell me quickly," Hunwold said, glancing around to see if any of his men watched.

"Master Hunwold, we have seen nothing of the enemy all day. And now in the darkness you have the advantage. You have a bright light all around you, while the enemy hides somewhere in the darkness. They will not dare attack from the shadows before dawn."

"That is my plan," Hunwold agreed. "We have fuel to keep the fires burning until daylight."

Wallen edged closer. Luthwin could see his hands shaking. "But what if the enemy should go away after you have burned the roofs of all your buildings? What if they wait for days until your men feel safe?" He had some plan, Luthwin knew. Trying to steady his voice, the slave youth continued. "I could go over the wall. I could find their encampment. And while they wait for daylight, you could surround them and force them to battle."

Hunwold went to the doorway of the shed and stood in the firelight, thinking. He turned slowly, his face in the shadows. "You might be seen climbing the wall," he warned. "It is a risk that I cannot protect you from. But if you wish to go, I will permit it."

Wallen clapped his hands softly. "I am not afraid. Does safety exist anywhere now? I am surely not safe inside the ton." He pulled his loose tunic in with his belt and tightened his leather leggings. "I will be back before it becomes light enough for them to see to attack."

Luthwin noticed that his father shrugged.

Like a shadow cast by the climbing smoke, Wallen dissolved into the darkness behind the smith shop. Luthwin listened. Not a sound rose above the noise in the courtyard. At least no one would stop Wallen before he slipped over the wall.

Back by the fire Hunwold called the men together. "We will rest with our weapons ready. My thanes will take the first watch and the last watch before dawn. Ceorls from my estates will watch from moonrise until we relieve them. Rest yourselves for battle. We may yet meet our enemy in the field."

"Ho!" someone scoffed. "They will slink through the brush and glens out of our sight to ambush us."

Luthwin lay down on the pavement near the fire, watching the flames subside. He pulled his sword close beside him and fingered its scabbard, thrilling to the feel of it. He would go to battle in the morning—his first battle!

When the thanes changed places with the ceorls, he awoke. The sounds of logs settling into the fires and men clanking in their ring mail as they turned in their sleep still filled the courtyard. Pillowing his head on his cloak, he slept again, not awakening until he heard his father's voice. He sat up.

Twenty thanes stood in a circle around Hunwold. "You all know why I trust the slave boy," he was saying. "I have sent him to find where the enemy is waiting. He will return before dawn. You are to help him coming back. Bring him to me as soon as he enters the enclosure."

Luthwin heard a low murmur. He shook out his cloak, put it over his shoulders, and got up. Standing beside his father, he waited. "The fires are dying down," the youth said finally. "Should I find something else to burn?"

Hunwold shook his head. "We will know soon what we will do. The men will watch carefully. They can see enough with the half moon shining now."

The moon climbed higher above the ton. The stars grew dim. In an hour, Luthwin thought, the east would show the first glow of morning. Listening for some sound outside the barricade, he walked down the space between the buildings and the wall.

Muffled voices made him stop. Leaning against a shed, Luthwin held his breath, "He has gone over to the enemy, no doubt," a thane muttered, "A Briton's blood is against all Saxons. I do not care what he has done in the past. Hunwold made a terrible mistake letting him go.

The old man is dotish about his son. He lets him sway his judgment. It was not so with the older two boys."

Luthwin stiffened. They were coming past him. "We had better be watchful," the other thane answered. "If the slave has betrayed us, he will wait for a time when all is quiet to do us harm."

The first man brushed his hands together. "I am a Saxon. I will not lift my hands to aid him." He reached threateningly for his sword. His companion nodded in the dim moonlight.

With soft steps of leather on duff and fallen thatch, they passed Luthwin and walked the length of the ton. Luthwin looked back to the watchtower. To his relief he saw Eldred sitting there. Eldred would obey his father whatever his own feelings.

The same two thanes returned. Luthwin remained motionless. They went by, muttering softly. He could not hear what they said. One man climbed the log barricade and peered into the level space around the wall. Seemingly satisfied, he dropped to the ground again, and they walked on. At the corner they disappeared. Luthwin heard someone talking in the courtyard. Perhaps they would stay beside the fire for a while. Climbing the side of a storehouse by the pegged ladder, he settled himself on a beam. He could see over the wall from there.

Moonlight flooded the green pasturelands above the ton toward the rough hills. Below he could see the straight shadows of furrow on furrow in the plowed ground. The road was empty. The black ravines wound like snakes through the hills to the river. The morning air was just beginning to move in soft puffs against his skin. Luthwin scanned the pastures for some movement. Wallen had little time left to return. Possibly the Britons had discovered him near their encampment. The Saxon youth wondered if they would spare him because he was of their race. But then Wallen would ask no favors of the enemy.

The guards came by again. Twice more they passed under him. And then he saw a faint dark spot moving along a line of bushes, advancing toward the ton. It came a few feet at a time, pausing, moving, waiting, darting ahead.

Luthwin watched the shape, only a part of a larger dark spot now, waiting on the far side of the wide-open area outside the wall. He is listening, Luthwin thought. The shadow stepped forward, then darted swiftly ahead with awkward steps. For a moment Luthwin wondered if the slave had gotten hurt.

His stride was different. He moved with a catch in his steps, not smoothly.

Suddenly Luthwin gasped. It was not Wallen, he was certain. The person paused just outside the barricade. A second later Luthwin heard him puffing as he climbed the earthworks. He looked at the watch-tower. Eldred did not move, but he looked in the boy's direction.

The guards had walked far down the wall. Luthwin scrambled down the side of the storehouse and leaned against the wall. On the outside, opposite him, someone rubbed the logs, feeling for a good place to climb. A rope fluttered above and caught on the end of an upright log. Feet thumped higher toward the top.

Luthwin silently drew his sword. The logs shook as someone pulled himself over. He dropped with a thud. Luthwin stepped behind him.

"Stop!" he commanded, his voice tense. "Turn around."

The dark mass turned. Luthwin did not need to see the face. He knew the hulking, habitually sagging shoulders.

"Luthwin. Master Luthwin," Brum whispered. "I have just now escaped from them. They have held me for two days, but I got away."

Brum's humble tone, the way he hung his head meekly, immediately made the Saxon youth suspicious. Luthwin held his sword firmly. Brum was strong enough to overpower him, but he must not call out for help now. He must let Wallen return quietly while the crowd of visiting thanes slept.

"I do not believe you," the Saxon boy said. "If you tell the truth at all, you will tell it to Hunwold. He is in the courtyard."

Brum took a step forward, reached his hand out once, then drew it back. Luthwin waited for him to go ahead toward the firelight. A few paces behind the slave, he followed. A second later he saw Brum feel in the side of his loose clothing. "Take your hands away from your sides," Luthwin commanded in a low voice.

Faster than he could have guessed, Brum spun around. In his hand a blade gleamed, long and menacing. "Lay down your weapon!" Triumph filled the slave's whisper. "Lay it down! Do you think I would be too squeamish to run this through you?" He laughed. "Not after doing my work and the work of your faithful Wallen while he hunted birds' eggs and went fishing with you. I think I will like my freedom when the Britons rule this place. I might be someone important myself for the services I have done them."

"You will have no freedom!" Luthwin gripped the hilt of his own sword, tightening the muscles in his arm for the thrust. "Do you think you can escape? All my father's thanes are patrolling tonight. And Eldred sits even now watching you from the tower. If he were not expecting someone else to come over the wall, he would call out now for the men to surround you. If you strike, he will know you are not my father's messenger."

Brum coughed, confused for a moment. "Then we will go between the buildings, out of his sight." He swung the sword in a steady, dangerous rhythm at his side.

"You are bigger than I am," Luthwin began. "And your sword is larger. I think you should feel safe if we walked side by side. I will not go ahead of you."

Brum sneered. "Do you, too, call me a bully?"

Luthwin stood still until Brum stepped toward a building. In the shade it cast he saw the Briton turn. Luthwin was ready. His sword caught Brum's just below his hand. He could tell by the way Brum handled the sword that he was not used to it. Momentarily off guard, Brum let the sword drop from his fingers.

Luthwin thrust again, near enough to make the slave boy back away. "Do not pick it up!" he warned. "It is not as easy as you imagine. I have had a lot of practice."

Brum watched him. Luthwin could read in his face his reluctance to give up. With lightning speed, he seized a pole leaning against the shed. In one vicious swing, he brought it across Luthwin's chest. The Saxon youth staggered, but did not fall. Instinctively he dodged Brum's second swing. Regaining his balance, he dodged again, struggling to catch his breath. Maddened, Brum flailed the pole. Luthwin drew him a step at a time out of the shadow of the building into the firelight.

"Who is that?" Hunwold's voice broke the quiet of the courtyard.

The slave froze, bewildered in the light. Luthwin touched his bruised ribs and decided none were broken. Stepping closer to Brum, he whispered, "Do not move!" In a louder voice, he called, "Come here, Father. I have someone who needs to talk with you."

Brum broke, darting between the sheds. He halted, desperately seeking another route. The passing guards blocked his path. Hunwold raised his spear.

"Halt!"

The Celt cowered against the shed, trembling. Luthwin dashed past him, picked up the ancient sword, and brought it to his father. Hunwold nodded. Without a word, he marched the slave into the courtyard.

Luthwin watched him go, then turned and went back to the wall. Wallen would be back in minutes. Leaning against the logs until he heard a stir at the end of the ton, near the Woden temple, Luthwin ran the length of the settlement.

Wallen stood at the center of the group. A thane held him roughly by one arm, shaking him while several others talked at once in threatening voices.

"Take him to my father at once," Luthwin ordered.

The guards turned around. "So this is your friend? Take him. I want nothing to do with a Briton!" one of them snapped.

Wallen followed Luthwin toward the courtyard. They stopped out of sight of the other thanes.

"I found them," the older youth whispered.

"Are there many?"

"A great number. They are in two groups."

Hunwold waited with Dedher and Elfric, two men he trusted most. Luthwin did not see Brum anywhere in sight and wondered for a moment if the slave knew something that might help Hunwold, and if he was willing to tell.

The eorl held out his hand and gripped Wallen's shoulder. "Now tell me quickly what you found."

"Picts are waiting near the ford," Wallen began. "I saw them first. They must have crossed after dark, for they were still wet and shivering. If they made a fire, you could see it from here." Hunwold pointed, and Wallen nodded. "And the Britons have banded along the glen, just past the spring planting of barley. Some of them sleep, but most of them are watchful."

"Did you see anyone posted to watch us?" Hunwold asked.

"No, not past the fallow ground."

With a whispered command to Elfric, Hunwold left. In moments the courtyard came alive with armed men moving as silently as the flickers of light playing on the buildings. Elfric took Wallen by the arm. "You must go with Hunwold in the battle. If you speak the truth more than the other lad did, you will be of value to him."

"Did Brum have something important to say?" Luthwin couldn't refrain from asking.

Elfric shrugged. "Your father will tell you about him later."

When Elfric stepped forward with his axmen, Luthwin leaned close to Wallen. "I have the old sword again. Do you want to take it? You cannot go into battle unarmed."

Wallen slipped the blade into a fold of his clothing. "I must be careful with no scabbard," he replied.

Luthwin walked ahead and joined his father. The gateman opened the great oaken doors for them. Like a stream of liquid flowing from a pitcher, they moved out into the early morning. Hunwold walked ahead, leading them to the ford.

"They think they will meet at dawn," he told his son. "We will wait until both Britons and Picts have massed on the field but are not yet organized to march. They may outnumber us, but we have better arms and more experienced warriors."

Luthwin felt a rush of pride as they marched.

His father looked at him with something like respect. "You saved us serious trouble when you caught the slave," he said. "Bitterness fills Brum, and he was up to no good."

Luthwin knew Hunwold would not speak of it again. He wondered what Brum would have done if he had not caught him.

Chapter Seven

LUTHWIN SPOTTED the enemy camping in a low spot at the end of the meadow. He guessed by the quietness of their camp that they did not suspect that the Saxons moved toward them behind the cover of the trees.

"We could beat them if we took them by surprise now," he whispered to Wallen.

Wallen shook his head, his fingers to his lips. "That would give the Britons a chance to attack the ton with no one there to defend it. Your father knows best. He wants to face them all at once when he knows where they are."

Luthwin nodded. He sensed the tenseness in the Saxon army. Above the line of trees on the eastern slope the sun lighted the sky now. In minutes the whole valley became visible.

The Britons started to move from the ravine into the meadow near the ford. Afoot and on horses they came, with just an echo of clattering armor and tramping feet reaching the waiting Saxons. Luthwin felt his heart pounding. Battle at last!

The two groups of the enemy milled together, the horsemen taking the lead. Under a scarlet banner the leader rode tall in his saddle.

Hunwold waited until the army had crossed half the meadow. Then when they had gone too far for them to turn back, he led his Saxons out of hiding. Swiftly his men marched across the grassland to meet the oncoming enemy. Luthwin saw the leader pause. His army bunched behind him, but he came forward again.

Luthwin marched with the foot soldiers behind Hunwold while the shield wall formed ahead of them. The Saxons made a sudden rush forward. Horsemen with spears galloped toward the Briton flanks; the shield wall moved ahead of the axmen. Like a storm shattering an unripe crop, they beat against the enemy.

Luthwin gazed in wonder as the Britons scattered, only to be driven back into a mass by the Saxon horsemen. The enemy's rear ranks broke and ran for the ford. Others turned in panic, trampling one another in their attempt to escape the Saxon army. Luthwin stood with his hand caressing his sword's hilt. The battle ended before he knew it was in its heat.

He looked across the meadow where hundreds of the enemy lay dead. The scarlet banner hung across a broken spear, still fluttering in the morning breeze. Their leader was dead. Was that why the Britons had fled so easily? he wondered.

He saw Elfric coming his way. "They were ill prepared," Elfric said. "If they had reached the ton as they planned, they would have had the arms they needed. Did you see, Luthwin, that only the first ranks had spears or swords?"

"But why would they attack without weapons?" Luthwin asked in surprise.

"One of your father's slaves has been collecting arms. But you spoiled their plan to assemble nearer the ton and receive weapons from his supply when you caught Brum returning with his message. The lad talks a great deal more than is wise." Elfric thrust his sword into its sheath. "Now that we know about the supply of weapons, we can be better prepared ourselves for future conflicts."

All the eorls who had come to Hunwold for protection from the Britons stayed to rethatch the buildings of the ton. Their retainers and thanes finished the buildings while the slaves rebuilt their daub and wattle homes. One slave family had disappeared. Luthwin did not want to know what had happened to them. He knew already what Saxon revenge could mean.

By midsummer, he thought, the ton would appear as it had looked before the attack. Only the great heap of stones in the meadow was different. Certainly now the threat of Britons in the Tweed Valley had ended.

Harvest came and passed. News arrived that Oswald was gathering his men. A messenger told Hunwold that the Northumbrian leader needed him now. The eorl prepared for battle again. Ceorls and thanes collected gear for the campaign. Slaves filled carts with food supplies.

"We are to meet the prince north of the Roman Wall," Hunwold explained to his wife after a feast in the great hall. He sat beside her on the raised part of the floor. Luthwin noticed the look of resignation on his mother's face.

Hunwold sat more erect than usual. "We will avenge ourselves for Raedfrith. Cadwallon himself will lead his army to meet Oswald."

Luthwin decided to make known his wish now. "Raedfrith carried the banner for Edwin, Father. May I carry Oswald's banner into this battle?"

His father's face turned grimmer. His mother shook her head, her eyes pleading with Hunwold.

"He owes his life to Oswald," Hunwold said at last. He raised his eyebrows as if uncertain what he should decide.

"I am able to carry it!" The youth leaned forward on his bench. "I am nearly fourteen years old." He looked from his father to his mother.

"He is too young," she objected softly.

But Hunwold reached to grip Luthwin's hand. "Your lot is cast with this prince's success. Bear his colors, if you must. You have made the choice, and may the gods protect you when the fighting is thick and death is near at hand."

They marched three days by the Roman road. Along a small river before they reached the Wall, they camped. The next morning other Saxon bands joined them. Finally, at evening, Oswald himself arrived with hundreds of soldiers he had raised while marching through Bernicia. Luthwin saw watchmen waiting on the hills above the encampment to signal the advance of the enemy. Around the camp others kept small fires ready to answer when the signals came.

Among Hunwold's men Luthwin walked, listening to their talk, the excitement growing with every hour that passed.

"It will be the greatest battle since the Saxon conquest," Eldred prophesied. "We must break this alliance between Penda and Cadwallon completely. There must be no union of Saxons with Celts!"

Another thane shook his head. "Everything depends on the

leadership of the two men. Cadwallon has rallied the Britons to resist their lords. For generations we have subdued or nearly wiped them out in some parts of the island. They have been separated in small hilltop settlements. Now Cadwallon has come up from Wales and brings them together with promises of power. If they lose their leader, the battle is ours, and the war is ours, too."

"What is Penda but an upstart trying to throw off the yoke Edwin placed on his shoulders?" spoke a third thane. "He has no bond of true friendship with the Britons, but only uses them to weaken his enemy."

"Aye. The alliance would fall to fragments if we destroy Cadwallon. We have seen ourselves how easily the small bands of Britons are overpowered. They do not have the same loyalty and discipline that a Saxon army has."

Eldred agreed. "They have been farmers on their rocky plots for so long that they have forgotten skills that are daily life for a Saxon."

A passing eorl stopped to listen. "Perhaps you men have not seen Cadwallon in battle," he suggested. "His strength and cunning would surprise you."

"We do not speak of Cadwallon, but of the roaming bands of Britons that have harassed us to the north," Eldred explained. "We, too, have faced Cadwallon and tasted the bitterness of his sword. Many of our number fell before him at Heathfield when Edwin died."

"Then may the God of Edwin and Oswald help us!" the eorl cried, leaning heavily on his spear. "I have not yet recovered from the wounds of that battle myself."

Luthwin slipped away through the groups of warriors. He must find Oswald yet tonight.

The prince sat with three eorls on a little rise near the river. Luthwin paused while he finished eating his oat cakes and milk. Oswald looked up and smiled with recognition.

"Come here, lad," he called.

Luthwin knelt at his feet and bowed his head. "I am happy to see you, my lord."

"And you have come to help me win my crown?" Oswald said. "I told you, Reud, that the lad would yet be of value to our cause."

Luthwin noticed for the first time the Briton beside him. He looked back to the prince. "I wish to carry your banner," he said. "My brother

Raedfrith fell at Heathfield carrying Edwin's colors against Cadwallon. I wish to go with you to carry the colors of victory over the enemy."

"If your father agrees, you shall!" Oswald's voice rang as he rose to take Luthwin's hand. "You shall indeed be the one to carry the banner into battle, and tomorrow you will see victory for Northumbria and for Christ!"

The prince's gaze searched the vast army camped around him. "Reud, see if we have Hunwold's permission to use his son."

Oswald sat down on a rock, and the great Briton went reluctantly to obey him. "Now, Luthwin, may I speak freely with you?" he began. "Were you not the whole winter under the care of the brethren on the island of Iona? Then perhaps you will understand, though you are but a lad."

Luthwin swallowed hard and nodded. Why was the prince confiding in him?

"You know that I take on this warfare as much for the sake of the cross of Christ as for my own kingdom. Cadwallon is a Briton—a Celt, if you please—but of the same race as our beloved brethren on Iona. His forebears were Christians of noble ideals, who carried the faith of Christ to Ireland. And later men of Ireland brought it to the lands of the Picts. Now Cadwallon has forgotten the faith and the mercy of true religion and has linked himself with a heathen."

Luthwin remembered what the Saxon thanes had said about the alliance earlier in the evening. How differently people looked at things. Oswald turned his fist in the palm of his other hand.

"I believe that Cadwallon has become even more fierce than Penda. That is what I hear on every hand. He who claims to be a Christian! In the name of Christ, we will meet him in the morning. And with the aid of God, we will have victory."

"But your army has few Christians," Luthwin objected. "The thanes will call upon Thor and Woden when the battle presses them. Can one army call upon two religions? Will the Christian God answer with help for us if He must share the allegiance of the army with other gods?"

Oswald shook his head. "Indeed, He is a jealous God, as the commandment says. But for the sake of those who believe, He will help." The princes eyes were piercing. "Luthwin, do you not believe what you heard while you studied with Brother Aiden?"

The youth remembered when Edwin's queen asked him that same question. What did he believe? "The religion of Aiden is a pleasant religion," he stammered. "But I have not learned enough. And all Christians do not live by the same teachings. At Edwin's court they did not observe the same Sabbath that Aiden teaches. And their worship was much more grand. Their bishop received great honor and wealth, but Aiden gave his shoes to a peasant. Which is the real Christian way? Why are Christians not all the same if they all follow the same leader?"

"Ah, you are right, lad." Oswald sighed. "If all men who claim to obey Christ would live as He taught, there would be no preparation for battle, for all men would live humbly without thirst for power or territory. All men would be brothers. All men would be sons of God."

Luthwin felt himself grinning. "Then it would be a strange world for a Saxon."

"Our race has lived far too long a way of bloodshed," Oswald said. "We must learn ways of peace and industry to build a strong nation with no enemies within or without. As long as men live as enemies, we will have want and turmoil. Living constantly with the threat of death gives nobody any happiness."

Thinking for a moment, Luthwin added, "What then will you do with Cadwallon when you have beaten him? If you do not destroy him and all his people, they will seek revenge for all the years to come. Even now they say they fight to avenge their forefathers who died by the Saxon sword."

"Someday we will all together make a new race of Englishmen, blended of Britons and Saxons, with one king and one faith."

Unable to keep from laughing at the idea, Luthwin asked, "The whole island united in one nation?"

"Not in my day, but someday." Oswald rose. Two eorls were coming to speak with him. "Be with me before dawn, lad," he called as the boy left.

Waving farewell, Luthwin went to his father.

That night, even with the watchmen posted, most of the men did not sleep soundly. The camp hummed with voices raised now and then to a low murmur. But always the current of whispers swept over the ground where warriors sat in groups or lay resting, ready for battle in their ring mail.

Dropping beside Hunwold, Luthwin stretched on the damp ground. Dew clung to his clothing. He shivered and sat up. His father slept, his bronze byrnie still under his head. Fog hugged the ground.

Luthwin got up and walked around the encampment. No fire blazed cheerfully where he could warm himself. The autumn chill reached to his bones until they ached. He wondered how long it would be until daybreak.

"Do not stray from the camp, lad," a warrior warned him. "The watchmen might mistake you for a Briton."

"I want to tramp around nearby," Luthwin said. "I am cold."

Ahead rose an outcropping of rocks. He could see in the moonlight where they dimly stuck out against the sky. He stamped his feet in the mossy earth to shake the water from his shoes, then climbed up the rocks and looked over the mist-filled valley toward the hills where the Roman Wall wound like a rope over the heathered earth.

Where would they face Cadwallon tomorrow? he mused as he sat down on a boulder. Somewhere not far away the other army also waited. Excited, he drew his knees up against him and tried to imagine the battle. Would he be able to forget the danger and hold the banner as he had asked to do? He did not feel so confident now that he had committed himself.

I am not yet fourteen years old, he thought. Yet tomorrow would mean the end of boyhood for him. Tomorrow he must have a man's bravery, a man's heart.

He heard the voices of men in the camp—muffled, hushed. He listened again. Nearer he heard another voice—the voice of one man that went on and on. He could almost hear the words. He leaned forward to peer over the rocks. There was someone on the other side.

Luthwin moved a step at a time—stopping, listening. He held his breath so that he could hear better. The voice sounded familiar. It is Oswald. He put his hand to his mouth. Had the prince heard him? He waited, motionless. Oswald continued.

"O God, my Maker, I am not a warrior"—the prince's words came low but clear—"but I have been given a warrior's work to do. I have neither the skill nor the wisdom to do Thy bidding. Show me Thy will and Thy way to do it."

The boy took another step. He could see the prince kneeling in the rocks, his head bent low, his hands clasped together.

"Help me to uphold Thy name and make it honored throughout my kingdom, and give me my just kingdom that I might do this work for Thee."

Oswald ended his prayer, but he did not get to his feet. His back stiffened as if he listened to something. Luthwin waited for some sound. The air was silent. Yet the prince tilted his head as though he heard a voice.

The fog shattered into long wisps of white floating near the ground. The moon broke through and shone on the prince. He raised his head and looked up.

"I thank Thee, my Father," he said, his voice little more than a whisper. He stood up and looked over his waiting army. Luthwin watched him walk back to his place among his personal thanes.

Would Oswald's God hear? Luthwin wondered. He wished that Aiden were there right then. Having that good man among them would change even the roughest warriors—just as Luthwin felt the change in his own heart as he listened to the prince's prayer.

At dawn Luthwin still lay awake, his mind exhausted from thinking. With the first stir in the camp, he was glad to be up. "I must be with Oswald from the very beginning of this day," he told his father as he munched thick slices of cheese and barley bread.

Hunwold inspected his spear and gave it back to him. "Ah, and your sword is already strapped to your side. I know, Luthwin, that you will behave yourself as a true Saxon today," he said. "And our people will remember with pride. Remember that, my son."

Luthwin sat on a pack and tightened the lacings of his leggings. He watched the men packing food and extra supplies to leave behind with the servants who would not go to battle. Then beside each eorl a small band of men lined up with shields and weapons ready for the march.

When he saw Oswald's thane with the standard, Luthwin jumped up and joined them. Reud unfurled it and set the shaft in the ground. "This is a proud banner," he said with feeling. He looked away, but Luthwin saw the tears on his deeply browned face. The Briton turned his shaggy head, his eyes bright. "You are honored, lad, to carry this. If I were not the best spearman in our band, I would carry it myself."

Luthwin nodded. He grasped the slender shaft with both hands and looked up at the strip of golden cloth fluttering above his head. He could not read the one word embroidered there, but that did not matter.

On horseback the army moved along the Roman Wall. Oswald's scouts had found the enemy in the night, and now they rode straight toward them.

Looking across the downs to a meadow, Luthwin saw Cadwallon's army. For a moment his heart fluttered as rapidly as the banner he carried. Could Oswald with his Bernician troops defeat the whole assembly of Britons and Mercians? Oswald had six thousand men, he said. But the enemy must have nearly twice as many. They filled the entire plain.

From the stir in the enemy camp, Luthwin knew they saw them coming. Leaders drew up their bands into battle formation. Steadily Oswald's army advanced toward them. On the last bit of high ground, Oswald raised his hands in a sign for the host to stop. He stood tall in his stirrups and addressed his men. "My God has shown me that we will conquer today in His name. We go to battle in the name of Jesus Christ. And He will strengthen us. May this day give you all faith!"

With a sweep of his right arm, he led the army ahead. They met the enemy on the open field.

Underneath him Luthwin felt his horse tremble with excitement and fear. He laid a hand on its neck. "Steady, Twi," he murmured. The horse whinnied and turned his head. With one hand on the standard to hold it straight, Luthwin pulled Twi closer to Oswald's mount.

Ahead surged the spearmen. Like hail driven by a fierce wind, their spears flew into the Briton ranks. The first Briton horsemen fell, but behind them another rank rushed on. Horses plunged, one rearing and coming down on another in wild confusion. Unseated riders took up their swords and dashed through the mass, swinging with deadly skill. Twi stood rooted like an oak where Luthwin held him. On his black horse Oswald sat erect, shouting orders to his thanes. His arm high, he signaled the axmen and infantry to follow. From the slope behind, a new surge of men swept down past Luthwin. The line of battle spread wider across the field, each man trying to press through the foe's shield wall.

Luthwin spotted a green banner. "Is that Cadwallon?" he cried.

A thane shouted an answer, but his voice vanished in the thunder of battle about them. Luthwin tried to watch both Oswald and the warrior under the green banner. His red cloak streaming behind him, his green leggings tight against his horse's sides, the Briton charged with his men.

The Saxon shield wall moved ahead, sometimes faltering and bulging as one group of men pressed on faster than their comrades could go. The youth saw the advancing Briton horsemen before the foot soldiers realized their danger. His throat ached from shouting. It did no good to call a warning. No one could hear.

Hurled over the heads of the Saxon infantry, the Briton spears penetrated deep into Saxon ranks. Against trampling horses, shields and swords offered no defense. The shield wall fell back in the middle, and all at once, the line broke. Briton horsemen, followed by the center of their army, swept through the breach. Oswald's voice thundered above the confusion.

Luthwin could hear no words, but he steadied the banner and held Twi.

The prince did not leave his position. Taking his own sword from its sheath for the first time, he struck at the Briton horseman that had come through the struggling thanes straight for him. The black horse reared. Oswald grasped the reins and struck at the rider again. The Briton fell from his saddle.

Around them Saxons formed a close defense to protect their prince. His arms aching, Luthwin pulled the staff of the colors from its leather strap and held it higher still so that all the Saxon army would see that their leader was there fighting. Now Luthwin could see beyond the immediate storm. Raging on every side, the Saxon army began to use its axes. The enemy drew away to let them have more room.

But as Oswald's guard spread outward, a new wave of horsemen rushed among them. Two Britons plunged on, wounded, but undeterred. Luthwin tried to warn Oswald. It was too late. His voice died on his lips. His heart turned cold as one of them threw his spear at a range too near to miss his mark.

Struck by the spear, the black horse stumbled, but Oswald jumped free. With careful aim he threw his own spear. Pulling an enemy weapon from where it stuck in the ground, he joined the foot soldiers.

"A horse for our prince!" Luthwin shouted.

An eorl heard him and jumped from his horse. Taking the offered animal, Oswald resumed his position beside the standard.

"Where is Cadwallon?" Oswald shouted. Luthwin scanned the enemy ranks. The green banner rushed with the horsemen to the left. The boy pointed.

"Strike where their leader is!" Oswald commanded.

The word passed down the line, and the left wing of the army moved ahead to meet Cadwallon's charge.

Luthwin settled the standard back into its strap and rested first one arm, then the other. Twi twitched his skin and pawed. The youth patted him.

"Cadwallon is moving back now," a thane called.

Oswald shook his head. "The battle may turn one way or the other very swiftly. He only pretends to lapse back. He will not give us ground yet."

Even as the prince spoke, the Britons swung in strong again, surrounding the end of the Saxon wing.

Oswald rode standing in his stirrups to direct his personal thanes. Through the army he rushed to meet the challenge. Luthwin held the banner and gave Twi his head. The horse seemed to know he must stay with the prince.

"Hold the line!" Oswald shouted. "If you rush ahead, you are lost!"

The Saxon army deepened its ranks, axmen lining up behind the strengthened shield wall. Beneath the shower of axes, the Britons fell back. Oswald led his men in a steady advance in a strong line. The Britons retreated still farther.

"They retreat too easily," Oswald warned. "Do not press in on them!" But the Saxons did not heed his command. Through a break in the Briton ranks they rushed, felling the enemy on either side. Luthwin saw the Briton flank sweeping down toward them. His ears echoed with the sudden savage war cry; his heart sank within him. He could see that the enemy had surrounded them.

He waited for Oswald's command, but the prince gave no order. Instantly Oswald dropped to the ground and grasped a broken piece of wood, then a longer piece from nearby. With the lacing from his leggings, he bound the two pieces of wood together.

Too quickly for Luthwin to keep up with him, he ran among the foot soldiers. On a little hummock of ground he stopped and held the two pieces of wood above his men.

"Has he gone mad?" exclaimed a thane next to Luthwin.

"No, it is the cross!" the youth shouted. He spurred Twi ahead through the men.

His head turned upward, Oswald spoke. His lips shaped the words of a prayer Luthwin could not hear. The prince's hands held the cross higher, and then he gave his command. "We will stand every man where he is." The army within hearing stiffened. "We will win. We will not fail. Let them press in on us. Fight where you are."

The prince's face shone with confidence that spread to his men. Luthwin sensed the sudden surge of strength and courage.

The youth looked around him. On every side the Britons advanced. Already the axmen and spearmen on the Saxon flanks met their blows. The green banner caught the breeze and spun out above Cadwallon's head. Luthwin jumped from Twi and drew his sword.

"I have so small faith, God, my Maker," he whispered. "But I do believe. Strengthen us!" He glanced at the cross in Oswald's hands. The Saxon army had no need now for the golden banner. He stood beside Twi, ready for the enemy to close in and crush them. But he was not afraid.

Chapter Eight

LUTHWIN DID not see what drove the enemy back. The Saxons stood ready to meet them, but they did not move out of the tight area where the Britons had surrounded them. Yet, the Britons retreated as if repelled by a vicious resistance. At last Oswald gave his signal.

His army swung out of its closed ranks and swept like a great ocean breaker upon the Britons. Luthwin saw die green banner again at the center of a small band of soldiers. The Saxons drove in toward it. And suddenly the banner fell. A terrible shout rose above the army. The Saxons charged on until the whole Briton throng broke ranks and ran. Horsemen followed the fleeing enemy, showering them with spears.

"Where is my horse?" Oswald's voice sounded calm in the sudden quiet as the action moved away.

Luthwin looked around. Only Twi stood nearby. The youth brought his horse to Oswald. "He is a small horse, but he is strong enough to carry you. I would be honored if my king would ride him."

"King!" Oswald repeated the word.

"Surely you will be king from this day onward!" Luthwin cried. "You have won over all your enemies and have saved your land from destruction."

The prince shook his head. "I have not won. My God has won. Luthwin, do you not have faith in Him?"

Luthwin glanced after the fleeing enemy. How could he tell the prince that he had just prayed for the first time? He looked back at the cross stuck into the ground and wondered. Surely two old pieces of wood held no magic. Oswald's God had heard because the prince had faith in Him. As Luthwin held Twi, Oswald mounted. Yes, in his own heart, the boy did believe!

The first of the Saxons rode back to the rise of ground where Oswald waited. Shout after shout rose from his men. "This shall be called Heavensfield!" Oswald declared. "For truly through Heaven's power we had this victory."

Another shout echoed his deep feeling. Then, strangely silent as if they did not know what to do next, the men heaped stones around the cross.

It was dark when the remainder of the army returned from pursuing the Britons. On a nearby hillside they camped. Tonight no mead or drunken shouting celebrated the victory. The vast host rested from exhaustion, small groups of men talking softly as if they thought of another enemy, one invisible, that might hear what they said.

Luthwin found his father's group. Without a word, he sat down and listened to their low conversation. He noticed that Eldred lay on a nearby stretcher where the fire could warm him. Another thane brought him something to drink, but the old man waved him away, then raised himself on one arm.

"I have seen today proof that we have worshiped false gods," Eldred said, his voice firm. He drew in his breath quickly, and Luthwin knew he was seriously wounded. "I wish to die a Christian, but there is none to baptize me. Must I go to the burning place that lasts forever as the bishop said?" He coughed and leaned to one side, his face grim with pain.

"I do not know what will come to you," Hunwold replied, standing beside his friend. It surprised Luthwin to see his father helpless and confused. "You have lived well, Eldred. You have lived long," Hunwold continued.

"But I have not lived by the way of Christ!" Eldred insisted. "I wish to die under His name."

The men in the circle around the fire looked at one another. No one seemed willing to say anything to comfort the old thane.

Are they all undecided even after today's victory? Luthwin thought. Why did not someone try to ease the dying man's mind?

Sigbert rose finally. "Die believing in the gods of our youth," he said.

"You have fought all your life a Saxon, believing in Saxon gods that came with our fathers from across the channel. Where is the strength of your courage? Die proud and brave!"

Eldred moaned and shook his head. "I have not lived by the faith of Saxon gods either, for they never helped me. I saw today that the Christian God is stronger to defend His faithful ones. Surely our king is one of His own."

Hunwold drew an armlet from his own arm. He laid it beside his friend. "I, too, saw the battle turn," he admitted. "Saxon strength did not deliver us. We fought our best, but we had made a fatal mistake of judgment. We allowed the enemy to surround us. Still, an unseen army enclosed us, an army that fought for us. I saw that, too, my friend."

"Then what must I do?" Eldred asked, his voice strong again. "There is not a bishop in all Northumbria."

"I have learned of Oswald's God from the good men at Iona," Luthwin answered, surprised at his own voice. "I will tell you what I know." He felt the eyes of his father's men on him. All at once he knew he must express his new faith.

His father took him by the shoulder and brought him to Eldred's stretcher. "Come, my son. Speak what you know."

Where should he begin? "I learned to pray," he said.

"No," Eldred interrupted. "Tell me. I want to know what I must do."

"You must believe. You must believe that God made the world and all of us. Aiden said that many times. And you must believe that Jesus Christ was God's Son, who came and died to buy us a life that lasts forever in a heaven place."

Luthwin's mind ran back over the stories his teacher had told him. He must think of something that would give Eldred confidence. "God is our Father. We are His sons, lost in a dark world. He searches for us and calls us to Him."

Eldred nodded. "Truly He has called to my heart today."

"We are like a coin lost in the dirt on the floor of the great hall. God looks for us in the way a woman searches for her gold piece if she loses it."

"But you have not yet told me about His Christ," Eldred broke in. He moved again, his face wretched with pain.

Luthwin tried to remember how Aiden described Christ. "Christ is our Brother," he began. "Like a true kinsman, He came to pay with His own life for our crimes. We have not honored heaven's laws. We owe the wergild, and it is so high a price that our lives must go to pay for it. Yet Christ paid it for us."

"That is according to Saxon laws," Hunwold said, looking at his men. "A kinsman may pay the penalty if it is too high for the guilty man."

The thanes murmured their assent.

"What then is this baptism the bishop told of?" a thane asked.

"It is a washing of the outside to show that the inside is clean because we believe," Luthwin said, not quite sure he was right. "Aiden said washing the outside of a cup does not make the inside clean. But God can clean the heart of any man who wants Him to wash him."

"That is what I wanted to know," Eldred said. "I believe. Now you can pray for me, Luthwin, for I do not know how to pray to this God."

Luthwin knelt beside the wounded thane, not knowing what to say either. "God, my Maker," he faltered, "we have no one to give Eldred the washing of baptism. But You can wash him clean in his heart. He believes in Christ. Forgive the price of his crimes against heaven's laws."

"Do I not make a sacrifice now?" Eldred asked when Luthwin got up.

The youth shook his head. "I never heard of any sacrifices. It is all paid for you."

Eldred died before morning. Because they did not know how to bury one who believed in Christ, his companions placed him on the downs with his armor and sword and raised a heap of stones over him, the way custom called for the burial of a Saxon warrior. The entire army marched back to the Roman road that day. The many wounded must rest. The dead must be buried. The leaders must make plans for the future.

While Luthwin ate his evening meal, a messenger came from Oswald. "The king wishes to see you," he said.

Hunwold nodded proudly. "You will receive a prize of battle from his hand for the service you did him."

Luthwin swallowed his bread and straightened his clothing. As he followed the messenger through the encampment, he trembled inside.

He knelt before Oswald.

The prince put a hand on each shoulder. "Lad, you behaved bravely in battle. Many a man twice your age turns weak in the terror of warfare. I wish to give you something that is precious to me. You may not prize it now, but I pray that you will learn to cherish it. Luthwin, did you learn to read at Iona?"

"Only a little."

"That is all the brothers could teach me, too," Oswald admitted. "I think perhaps I was too preoccupied with thoughts of my homeland to be a good pupil. Or perhaps I was too old, or feared for my family. Anyway, I did not remember the few words they taught me."

From his cloak he took a small roll of parchment. "But I know these words in my heart," he said. He untied the leather shield and opened the parchment.

"In the beginning was the Word, and the Word was with God, and the Word was God. The same was in the beginning with God. All things were made by him, and without him was not anything made that was made. In him was life; and the life was the light of men." John 1:1–4.

Luthwin looked at the beautifully written copy. His gaze traced the gold letters on the purple parchment with wonder.

"What, then, is the Word that in the beginning made the world? Did not God make everything?"

Oswald smiled. "The Word is Christ, who is God's only Son. He came as a messenger, and as the message, too, for He by His life told us how men ought to live. It was He who made the world in the beginning, for He is one with His Father."

"I did not know that to tell Eldred," Luthwin said. Wondering if he had spoken the truth to the old man, he decided to ask the king about it.

Oswald listened to all he said about Eldred. "Surely God heard your prayer and accepted him," he commented. "He is a God of mercy and love and will accept any who claim His words."

During the following days the army marched through Bernicia. At Bamburg, Oswald had established his household. There all the warriors of his kingdom gathered for his coronation. Luthwin felt a thrill of pride when he saw the thin circle of gold on Oswald's head. Now his friend was really a king.

"I wish my people to become Christians," Oswald said when he addressed them in the courtyard of his villa. "You have been witnesses of the power of the true God. Do you not believe?"

Many shouted their agreement. Some who had accepted the faith under Edwin remembered their vows and promised before their king and all his men to again leave their long-held heathen worship.

"We need a teacher." Hunwold's voice echoed through the courtyard of Bamburg. "How can we follow the ways of this religion until we know the path? Can you not call someone to teach us the ways of the Christian faith?"

"Aye!" The exclamation came low and fervent.

"I will send for a man wise in the Scriptures," Oswald promised. "The Christian brothers who helped me in my exile will help us all now."

Bamburg lay a short distance from Hunwold's estate. The next evening Luthwin sat beside the fire in the great hall at home, listening to the men recounting the entire campaign. While clouds of smoke twisted through the beams and out the openings at the ends of the roof, he thought of his first battle. He could tell his children about it someday, and he would remember for the rest of his life the king standing amid the struggle, holding the cross high.

His father interrupted his thoughts. "Luthwin, why did you not tell us of the Christian faith when you returned from the land of the Scots?"

Luthwin gulped down the lump in his throat and felt his cheeks burning. Why had he remained quiet? Had he been ashamed to tell of what he had learned? Did he have any excuse at all?

"Aiden did teach me the words of this faith. But what he said did not change my heart. I listened because he told stories that passed the long winter hours. I think I did not really believe myself until I heard Oswald pray before we went to battle. When I heard him talking to his God so confidently, I could not help myself. I believed Someone heard him and would come to his aid."

Luthwin told the men what he saw on the eve of the battle.

"He has power from heaven, as he said. Well can we call the place of victory Heavensfield," Hunwold said.

He called for the food, and Luthwin's mother brought it herself, helping the slave serve each person in the hall. She smiled at Luthwin, pride brightening her eyes.

The next day Luthwin showed her the little parchment scroll.

"It is beautiful!" she exclaimed. "What delicate animals and birds and flowers! A great artist must have done this."

Luthwin laughed. "All the brothers at Iona do fine work like this. Each day they spend an hour copying from the large scrolls, making others so that more people may have the Scriptures to read."

His mother looked at him with a new respect on her face. "You did not tell me. Did you learn to read at Iona, my son?"

Luthwin held his parchment up. "In the beginning was the Word," he began. He could not remember what came next, and he could not read the next word. "I learned just a little. But I will learn to read from the teacher who comes." He placed the scroll inside its sheath and gave it to his mother. "Keep it safe for me until I can read it all."

"May not a woman learn to read, too?" she asked.

"I have heard that Christian women gather in schools," Luthwin said. "But I doubt we will have a school in Bernicia for a long time."

"Then I will be content keeping the writing for you." His mother wrapped it carefully in a length of woolen cloth and put it in her oak chest.

"I will teach you what I know of the religion of Christ," Luthwin promised. He did not feel shy talking with his mother. "And when the teacher comes, we will go to Bamburg to hear his words."

"We will invite him to come here, too," his mother added. "We have much hospitality to repay after the brothers cared for you for so long."

Only a few weeks passed until the teacher came from Iona. A messenger brought the news that he taught at Oswald's court. Hunwold took Luthwin. But they came home in a few days disappointed.

"He speaks beyond my understanding," Hunwold told his wife in the great hall that evening. "I heard with my ears what he said, but my heart could not follow the language. He is a learned man, perhaps; and he speaks the Saxon tongue with skill. But he is not the man to teach us."

Luthwin talked to Wallen about it later. "I wish they would send Aiden," his Celtic friend said.

The Saxon youth shook his head. "I know he would be happy to come. He told us so. Do you remember? But he did not learn to speak our language well enough to speak to the people."

"But we could translate for him," Wallen suggested, grinning.

Luthwin felt the idea bursting like a milkweed seed from its pod. "Could we?"

"I had to translate for you before all the Celtic words came easy for you."

They both laughed when they remembered. He had felt foolish, Luthwin remembered, when he had to repeat the Saxon words over and over for the wise teacher. "We could do it!" Luthwin said with real conviction. If only he could think of some way to make sure Aiden would come! But it was a long journey across the heathered downs to the coast and Iona. They would have to wait and see.

But he could pray to God to send his old teacher to be their missionary. And he did. Again and again he found a quiet place and begged the favor. At last he felt sure God had heard his prayer. A new confidence filled his heart.

But he had one more matter to take care of—something he could do to show his faith. He waited for just the right time to speak to his father. "I have thought about the next teacher," he said one evening. "Perhaps he will not know the Saxon speech."

"That is true," Hunwold agreed.

"Then could not Wallen interpret for him?" Luthwin watched his father's face. "He speaks both Celtic and Saxon."

Hunwold frowned. "We owe the boy a great deal, Luthwin, for the faithful service he has given. But you must remember that he is still a servant, and we must treat him in a fitting manner. You must learn to maintain your dignity as the son of an eorl, for someday you will take my place as head of this family and this settlement. I fear I have been too careless letting you spend so much time with your slave. He does not fear you as he should."

Luthwin said no more. Another time he would speak again. He walked around the ton wondering what made the difference between the two races that lived here within the barricade of logs. More than half the people were his father's property. The others worked for him part of the time in return for the protection he gave them. Nothing but the tradition of conquest could explain the slavery of the Britons.

If I had been captured in battle, he thought, I might be a slave to some Briton family now. The idea shook him. His father's decision did not satisfy him. Someday when he was lord of his father's lands, Wallen would be a free man. Until then they would remain faithful to their friendship.

Chapter Nine

EVERYWHERE THE Tweed Valley came alive with spring. The snow squalls of winter had passed. In the forests and meadows of Hunwold's lands grass sprouted new and green through the old brown of last year's growth. Birds flew back. The fields smelled warm in the sun.

Luthwin ran up the road from the ford, waving to the gateman. "I have good news! Father's favorite horse has foaled!"

"And I have better news," answered the gateman. "But Hunwold would like to tell you himself. Go to the hall, and you will see for yourself."

Luthwin looked at his hands and arms, all covered with dirt from the field. "Just a moment," he panted. First he paused at the well to splash water from the tub on his face and arms. He gave his arms a shake, then still dripping, he entered the great hall, only to stop suddenly and back out. His father had guests. Maybe, he thought, he should change his clothing before he went in before them.

"Come in, my son!" Hunwold's voice rang out. "Our guest is eager to see you."

Luthwin wiped his face on the sleeve of his shirt. Slowly he walked inside. For a moment he could not see who sat beside his father on his raised platform. He blinked away the sun spots still dancing in front of his eyes.

"My prayer is answered!" he whispered finally. Gladness flooded him.

"Then you have been praying?" Aiden's voice was warm with friendship. "If you have been praying as you say, then my prayers for you are answered as well." He lapsed into Celtic words Luthwin only half understood.

Have I already forgotten all the Celtic language I learned? Luthwin thought.

"He has told me," Hunwold said, "that he had first to see you on his way to Bamburg and King Oswald. The good brother must stay with us to partake of our board tonight. The day is too far spent for him to reach Bamburg before darkness."

Luthwin searched for Celtic words to explain. At last Aiden understood. He smiled, his face radiant.

"Ah, and where is your friend Wallen?" he asked.

"He plants in the field today. Shall I call him?"

Aiden glanced through the door at the low sun. "No, he will come in soon. But I do want to speak with him. Does he too believe?"

Luthwin caught his breath, embarrassed at the pointed question. "I do not know," he admitted.

Aiden's gentle face clouded, disappointment showing in every line. "Then you have not spoken to him of Christ?"

"He always wishes to speak of something else," Luthwin began, searching for some excuse. "I cannot speak well of such things. I know only what he also heard."

Aiden reached to grip his hand. "You have learned to know Christ well enough to speak to Him and call upon Him for help. That is a great deal. Now that your heart is open, you will learn quickly. God bless you, Luthwin." He turned to Hunwold. "I cannot tell you all you wish to know, or all I wish to say. But I do want you to know the true God."

"Surely we will all come together to listen to your words tonight," Hunwold said. "But first you must refresh yourself at my table." He nodded toward the door where Ceda stood with the first of the feast she had made.

Aiden understood. The thanes entered quietly. At once Luthwin realized he must do something. He slipped from the hall and rushed to his mother.

"At Iona they drink only water or milk," he said. "You must not bring mead into the hall. Brother Aiden will not drink it, I am sure."

His mother looked at the tall flask of mead in her hands. She set it down and called to Ceda.

"I have fresh milk from this evening's milking," Ceda said with a smile. "We can carry all that the company can drink, but what will the men say? They have not tasted milk since they were children."

"We wish to please our guest," Luthwin's mother insisted. "I will speak to Hunwold's thanes. Thank you, Luthwin, for telling me. You may go back to your place beside your father now."

In the place of honor across from Hunwold, Aiden sat in the tall oak chair. Between them the fire flamed up. Loaves and cheeses and small cakes of finest oat flour rested in piles on the table. Honey and dried fruits were plentiful.

Luthwin watched his mother enter with Ceda. While the slave woman held the great jug, she poured milk into Aiden's cup. When she poured for the first of Hunwold's thanes, he looked up, his face showing surprise as the white stream flowed into his cup. He raised his eyebrows and looked from one of his companions to another. The lady served them one at a time, bending to whisper to each as she went. Some smiled with understanding. Others drank the milk with sober, unhappy faces. Luthwin could not help smiling to himself at their dour expressions.

Aiden stood up. "God bless all in this house, and all we eat with grateful hearts in Thy presence." The missionary seated himself, his hands folded in his lap.

"It was Edwin's custom to bless food," Hunwold told Luthwin.

In spite of all the food before him, Luthwin felt too excited to eat his fill. He could not help comparing the teacher with the Roman bishop who had sat in the same chair of honor nearly two years before. Aiden's clothing was worn and plain. He had no chains of gold or any ornaments, nor did he carry so much as a purse. But more than the difference in clothing was the contrast in the two faces. The bishop had determined, haughty lines about his mouth. He had been impatient and demanding. Now Aiden sat there, his smile genuine, his hands quiet. He ate gratefully of what was given him and asked for nothing more.

"How long the thanes take in eating tonight!" Luthwin thought. Would they never finish filling their plates? He was relieved when

Hunwold motioned for Ceda to remove the food.

The eorl raised both hands, signaling his men to listen. The room hushed. "We will be the first in all Bernicia to hear the words of this teacher," he said. "It is he who took care of my son while he waited through the winter in the land of the Scots. I have heard good things of this man. Listen with open minds to his teachings."

Aiden stood. His eyes swept the room and settled on Luthwin. "I speak your language so poorly, and I have so much to tell you," he began. Luthwin knew what he wanted.

"He needs Wallen," Luthwin told his father in a whisper. "Wallen could help him now."

Hunwold placed his hand to his lips. And Luthwin said no more.

"I will try to speak the good news that rests on my heart." Aiden shaped each word separately, unsure of himself.

Hunwold leaned toward his wife and spoke softly. She left the hall. In a moment she returned with Wallen. His head bowed, the slave boy walked to Aiden's side. Luthwin half heard the few Celtic words Aiden said. Then the teacher looked at Hunwold with gratitude. Wallen repeated his thanks in the Saxon tongue. Then smoothly the two of them began Aiden's message.

"God has bidden me bring you news of His love for you. I will tell you a story from the Scriptures, for it is by the Word of God that you will learn of Him.

"A great lord prepared to go on a journey in the service of his king. He called his servants to him and put them in charge of his fields and all that was his. 'I will pay you well for your services,' he said. 'Your share will be part of all that my estates produce while I am away.'

"In the season of harvest, the lord thought of his property. 'I will send men to collect the products of my land,' he said.

"But when the men reached the lord's lands, the servants beat them and sent them away, saying, 'We will not deliver to the lord his share of the crops.'

"Again the lord sent other men. The servants killed them. And finally he sent his only son." Aiden paused. Luthwin had heard the story once before, but he waited for the teacher to continue. "The wicked servants killed the son as well, for they thought to take all his inheritance for themselves."

Luthwin looked at his father. Hunwold leaned forward, his face showing his interest. He glanced at Luthwin and nodded. Aiden spoke again, and Wallen repeated his words for the Saxons.

"You have seen great warfare, my friends. Your homes and cattle have been ravaged by struggle. You have seen servants turn against their lords and refuse them what is their due. But all men are servants of the God who made them and this earth."

Luthwin listened as Aiden explained the rebellion of mankind. "But God is not like man," the teacher continued. "A man says in his heart that he can forgive his friends who are at his table or who suffer the hardships of battle side by side with him, but his enemy he will hate.

"While we were His enemies, God loved us. He sent His only Son to pay our ransom with His own life. And still we refused to give the worship that belonged to Him. Now we have only to believe to become sons of God and adopted heirs of His kingdom."

Hunwold lifted his hand. "Ah, then how does one walk the Christian way?"

"You will learn to love God by serving your fellowmen. Do unto all men what you would wish them to do to you. Give without grudging, for each man is your brother, purchased by Christ and redeemed from death to eternal life."

"And what are the laws of heaven?" Hunwold asked again.

"Do not kill. Do not steal. Do not give witness to falsehood or treachery. Be content with what is your own. Be clean and honest and faithful in all matters. Love God above all else, and worship Him only." Aiden smiled. "The laws of God are not harsh laws, but make the doer glad in his heart."

"These are wise laws," Hunwold agreed. "A man would live well by obeying them."

"You do not speak of allegiance to the Father in Rome," a thane observed as he stood up. "The bishop who visited us before spoke of the Roman Father, whom we must obey in all things."

Aiden listened to Wallen's translation. "Sir," he replied, "God is our Father. To none other do we owe worship or obedience in matters of faith. The bishop who came from Rome spoke from a convicted heart, I am sure. But he did not find authority for such claims in the Scriptures."

Aiden reached for a parchment folder. He held it high so that everyone could see. "Your youth must learn to read the Word of God. It is the only way one can know what is God's will. Then you may have parchments of your own to study when no teacher is with you. God Himself will be your Teacher if you can read the message He has sent you."

Luthwin stared at the beautiful copy Aiden held. It was as large as the platter on which Ceda carried bread, and letters covered it.

"You must have a school in Bernicia," Aiden said.

Luthwin's mother bent forward. "Then you shall learn to read even more than the words on your small parchment, Luthwin."

He nodded.

For hours the thanes listened with respect, asking the teacher questions that troubled their minds. Twice a slave brought more wood for the fire. But at last Hunwold stopped the talk. Everyone could see Aiden's weariness.

All night Luthwin lay thinking about what he had heard.

Early in the morning the Celtic teacher prepared to leave for Bamburg.

"We will certainly come to hear you at the king's court," Hunwold promised. "But first we must consider all we have heard here."

Spring saw no preparation for war as had taken place for years past. With the death of Cadwallon, all the Britons settled back quietly on their own lands. The Picts remained north of the Tweed. Hunwold could spend all of his time building up his ton and clearing new land for the plow. Slaves might fell the trees and work the land, but a Saxon with his own hands must build his walls and houses.

Luthwin learned to square timbers as supports for another new building. "Father, why do we not use stones as the people of York did in their church?" he asked.

Hunwold threw back his head in scorn. "Wood is the building material of the Saxons. We will not have our walls falling in on us, or our roofs pressing down. We cut living trees and shape them as pleases us. That is our way."

It was true that stone made a cold, unfriendly building. But Luthwin remembered Edwin's small stone chapel. It combined wood and stone into a nice structure. He wondered if James the deacon had come back to it now or if the war had destroyed Edwin's whole villa.

The youth looked forward to the evenings around the fire in the great hall. The thanes still talked about Aiden's visit. Luthwin knew they were divided in their decisions. Ten spoke out boldly for the new faith and said they wished to be baptized when the teacher returned. Some said they wanted to wait until they heard more before they decided.

"Let us see if this man lives himself what he teaches," several said. "We do not wish to make fools of ourselves following a false teacher."

Sigbert refused to listen to any new teachings. "I am a Saxon. I will live as my father's lived," he insisted. "The old ways are true ways, for they have stood for hundreds of years. Only truth could stand that long. I will not dishonor the creed by which I have always lived."

But Luthwin saw him once tracing letters of some kind on a tablet of wood. Luthwin had seen runes before. He expected to see a line of the ancient marks when he looked at the tablet later. But the letters were different.

"I think he is trying to cast a spell on you," Wallen commented when Luthwin told him about the incident. "Sigbert has great faith in the power of writing to cast spells for evil or good. He thinks all writing is magic."

"I used to think so, too," Luthwin remembered. "Do you still have the old sword?"

Wallen grinned. "Of course, I still have the sword. But do not speak so loudly. Someone might hear."

"It has some writing on it," Luthwin said.

"Do you suppose the letters on it are runes?"

Luthwin wondered about it for several days. "Why do we keep puzzling?" he asked Wallen one afternoon. "You bring the sword to the creek. I want to see just what kind of writing the marks are."

When Wallen brought the sword, they took it from its scabbard and examined it from hilt to point. "I never noticed before that the hilt has this shape," Luthwin said. "It resembles a cross."

"We have polished most of the figures away," Wallen commented, running his fingertips over the blade where the letters had been. "I can feel just the faintest lines, but I cannot see them at all."

Luthwin took the weapon, holding it to the sunlight so that he could see better. "The letters look like the ones Aiden taught us," he said.

Neither of them could read the words. Wallen put the sword back in its scabbard and returned it to his hiding place. "I may need it someday." He laughed. "You know, Reud used to be a slave, and now he is a trusted warrior of Oswald."

Luthwin felt a pang of sadness. "But I am not a king. And I may never be an eorl." He had been thinking for a long time about his future. The Christian God was calling him softly, as if He had some special purpose in store for him.

Wallen smiled reassuringly. "I would not be happy thinking always of battles. I like to work outdoors in the sun better than to sit all day talking in the hall. Outdoors I can sing while I work and look at the sky and the hills. That is better."

"We will always be friends," Luthwin promised. "And someday you will no longer be a slave."

Hunwold began building a wooden chapel. Along the barricade to the west of the great hall it rose with hewn logs for walls. Now the beams went into place, and Luthwin helped each day.

"When Aiden comes again, we will have a baptism in the Tweed," Hunwold explained one day. "And we will need a place for the believers to worship the true God."

Sigbert stood back from the building, his eyes smoldering with anger. "You did not rebuild the temple of Woden after fire burned its roof and beams months ago." He pointed a trembling hand to the rain-soaked walls beginning to sag on their foundation at the other side of the enclosure. "You are to blame for this desertion of the ancient gods!"

Hunwold eased down the timber he held. "You yourself were too busy at the time overseeing your fields to help me," he reminded the priest. "And you know well that feasts were all that brought the whole community together to worship with you. Often you had to threaten in order to get them to bring their sacrifices."

Sigbert shrugged, but he still glared at Hunwold. "Where the leader is indifferent, the people become so."

Hunwold looked away as if he had not heard. Soon Sigbert left.

"Why is Sigbert so determined to remain pagan when all have seen with their own eyes the evidences that the Christian faith is the true religion?" Luthwin slid out on a beam to pound harder on a peg to hold it to the support under it.

"He has had good profits from exacting religious fines and duties from my men," Hunwold said. "He is bitter because so few pay heed to his voice. He now has little power over the ton, where before the men feared him and his magic."

"When I was small, it frightened me to see him coming on his big white mare," Luthwin admitted. "He never smiled and always looked terribly fierce."

Hunwold laid down his hammer. "In the old religion we had to buy favors from our gods with gifts and sacrifices. They would become angry and withhold blessings, it seemed to us, if we did not honor them this way. But they are dead gods. They are nothing more than the inventions of men's hands, just as their temples are."

A thane came to his father and whispered something. Hunwold climbed to the ground and disappeared. Luthwin finished pounding the peg deep into its hole and followed him until just outside the hall he heard his father's voice.

"It is probably only words," Hunwold said.

Several men stood around him looking grim.

"He has always made threats," Wilfrig said. "But he may do as he says. Never have I seen Sigbert so angered."

"The Christian God can protect His own house," someone said. "We need fear no man wild with rage."

"He may bring harm to the whole ton, not just to the church," Dedher objected, shaking his head. "He is like a man without reason these days."

"He says misfortune will come to Hunwold's household because he has forsaken Woden," another warned. "If his words come to pass, we will know that he does indeed speak the truth."

"Misfortunes come to all men!" Dedher scoffed. "Does the Christian faith claim to turn away all sickness and trouble from those who obey its creed?"

"We will see." Elfric walked away.

What misfortune could trouble Hunwold's household now? Luthwin wondered. The crops were growing well. The ton had expanded its walls and earthworks, and all the thanes and ceorls had more than they had ever owned before. And no enemy threatened to invade Bernicia now.

The next day he told his mother about the conversation when he visited her bower.

"Do not be alarmed," she said. "Sigbert is a man of many words and few deeds. He was eager for battle when Hunwold joined Edwin, for he needed more livestock, and he thought he would exact offerings. He prophesied a great victory then."

She put her needlework aside and walked to the unshuttered window.

"Luthwin, we have not had fish for many weeks now. You must go fishing in the river today. Just last night someone said in my hearing that he was hungry for fish. And this is a good time of year to catch them. Ceda will give you food to eat while you are gone."

Luthwin looked at the soft haze filtering the sun. Everything outdoors was warm and bright, inviting him. "I would like to go if I could take Wallen with me to help."

His mother sighed. "Why do you wish to spend your time with a slave's son? You ought to make friends with the sons of thanes and the other eorls. It is because your own brothers were much older, too old to be real companions to you, I suppose. Well, your friend is busy with the overseer today, Luthwin. You must go alone."

Luthwin found the nets in the storehouse and got some oat cakes from Ceda. Only an hour later he had ridden far upstream, past the homes of several ceorls and the last enclosure, where an old thane lived part of the time.

In the tall grass beside the gate Luthwin noticed a horse tethered. It was strange, he thought, for the old man to have a new horse now, for no trader had passed by for a long time—and a white horse at that.

Luthwin hurried Twi to a place where some rocks stretched far out into the river. Here he left the horse to graze while he drew out the net. Walking gingerly on the wet stones, he swung the net into the stream and let the current float it out and swirl it to midstream.

When he pulled the net in the first time, he had caught two small fish by the gills. Over and over he flung it out into the river. The pile of fish at his feet grew. At noon he ate the oat cakes. After resting his arms awhile, he started fishing again. It would take a large bag of fish to feed the men who ate each day in the great hall. And he must have them back in time for Ceda to prepare them for supper.

Suddenly a noise on the bank startled him. He turned around quickly.

"Master Luthwin." Sigbert dismounted, his white mare standing at the edge of the water. The priest stepped onto the rocks. "You have a good catch, I see."

Luthwin tried to suppress his mounting wave of apprehension. "My efforts have been rewarded with blessing today."

Sigbert bent over the pile of fish. He cleared his throat and straightened, smiling crookedly, unnaturally. "How came you to go fishing today?"

Luthwin wondered why he asked. "My mother said she heard someone at table say he was hungry for fish."

"Aye!" Sigbert clapped his hands with satisfaction. "It is the right time to have fish. The streams are full of fresh water, and cold." He glanced toward the rapids foaming below where they stood. "This is a dangerous place to choose for fishing, Master Luthwin."

The youth laughed aloud. But he knew his effort to appear confident sounded false. "This is where I always fish when I have time to come so far. There is good fishing from these rocks."

"Yes, it is too far for you to call for help if you should have the misfortune to lose your footing on the slippery rocks."

Luthwin's eyes dropped to his feet, then darted back to Sigbert. The heathen priest had planted himself between him and the shore. The boy gripped the net, the palms of his hands cold, his heart pounding. Sigbert's eyes narrowed, and he no longer pretended to be friendly.

A step at a time he walked out on the rocks. "You were the one who started all this talk," he said, his voice high with anger. "When you babbled to Eldred when he was too fevered to know what he said, you made him believe. He was weak and dying. Now you have drawn away the people of the ton. You shall pay, Master Luthwin."

He lunged forward. Luthwin had nowhere to go but backward. Stepping too far, he fell with a splash into the icy water. Shivering, he still held the net. The current swept him toward the rapids. Above the roar of the water he could hear the priest shout.

"God, my Maker," Luthwin prayed, "preserve my life!"

Chapter Ten

TWICE LUTHWIN struck a rock beneath the surface of the water, but he was too numb to feel bruised. He gripped the net as if he held a line to the shore, and suddenly it jerked taut. The current pulled his body, but the net held him, bobbing like a stick in the swirling water. Shaking the water from his eyes and dripping hair, he tried to see.

Stifling the instinct to cry for help, Luthwin waited for Sigbert to vanish around the bend in the trail. After reaching with his feet for something beneath him, he pulled himself hand over hand upstream toward the end of the fishing net.

There may be rocks close to the surface, he thought. His arms ached; his body throbbed with cold. It seemed a mile to shore; but if he had a rope, he knew he could throw it far enough to reach the crags at the edge of the water. He began to wonder how long he could hold the net—even if he reached where it had caught.

The sun was low. He had been in the water for a long time. The fishes he had caught still lay where he had piled them. On the bank somewhere Twi still grazed, for he could hear the horse nipping grass. Luthwin marveled that his hands clung to the net though he could hardly feel the cords around his fingers.

"Twi!" he called. "Come, Twi!" He heard the horse moving through the tangle of brush toward the water. But what could Twi do?

An inch at a time, Luthwin worked himself along the net again, clinging with his last desperate strength against the swiftness of the current. Below the rapids, water pounded the rocks. Upstream other rapids roared. His head was dizzy.

The sun disappeared over the wooded hillsides. Darkness followed quickly. With his feet Luthwin felt the firmness of a rock under him at last. He settled one foot on either side of it, holding himself enough to rest his arms a little.

Probing under the water, he felt for the end of the net and found it, tangled in the sharp edges of the rock. He could go no farther toward safety. Settling his head on his arm and trying to think what he should do, he wondered if he had any hope of rescue.

In the darkness he looked at the sky where stars glimmered. If he had just a small light, he would feel better. With just a little light he would not feel so alone.

"God, my Maker," he whispered, "You have caught me here and saved me from immediate death. Hold me here! Help me!"

He tried to think of the words Aiden spoke in the great hall. He thought of stories from the Scriptures he had heard in the small stone hut on the island of Iona. He thought about his own little parchment with its letters of gold.

"In the beginning was the Word." He could remember that much. Oswald said the Word was Christ, that He was God's Son and God's Message to all men to show them how to live.

Luthwin remembered the laws that Aiden repeated in the great hall to his father's thanes. "Do not kill." That was a law of heaven. "I have not killed," he thought. "My new sword has never drawn blood, though twice I took it to battle." For the first time he felt glad he had not had the chance to fight against the enemy.

He longed for a light. Again he tried to rest his arms, but he could no longer grip the rock securely with his feet. He tried to pray.

"In him was life; and the life was the light of men." The words—the last words on his parchment—came to his mind one at a time. He said them over and over.

"His life is light!" Luthwin whispered. "His life shows the way through darkness. A man must follow His light." He felt more comfortable now, even with a cold wind blowing on his arms, even with the current pulling at his body.

In the darkness Twi whinnied to him. He called, and the horse stepped cautiously down the bank, stopping to whinny again when stones stirred by his feet rattled down ahead of him.

"Careful, Twi."

The horse stood there waiting, afraid to step into the current.

Luthwin strained his eyes to see him, but he could only hear him there, breathing and snorting. Then he saw a flicker in the trees. It bobbed along, growing brighter. He wondered if Sigbert was coming back to make sure he had drowned, or was it someone coming with help? Luthwin shifted his hands on the net and pulled himself higher out of the water to see.

A torch flared up not far down the path. Twi whinnied and started climbing up the bank.

"Luthwin?" Wallen's voice came out of the darkness.

"Here!" Luthwin was surprised at the hoarseness of his own voice. "Wallen, come down. I am in the water!"

The Celtic slave stepped down the rocks to the edge of the river. "I do not have a rope. Is there a rope on Twi?"

"No!"

Wallen swung his torch around. "Maybe I can find a fallen sapling long enough. You are not far out in the deep water."

"Hurry," Luthwin begged. Suddenly he felt too weak to hold even a few minutes more.

In no time Wallen held a pole across to him. With one hand Luthwin let go of the net and gripped the pole. Then he held it with both hands, almost unable to feel the pole because of their numbness. Wallen backed out of the shallow pool where he stood and towed Luthwin toward shore. Luthwin felt his feet touch a solid bottom. At last the current around him slowed, and he could stand by himself.

A moment later he leaned, shivering, against Twi, his arms around the horse's neck. "God sent you," he told Wallen.

Wallen coughed awkwardly. "I know," he said.

"You will have to get my fish." Luthwin took the bag from around Twi's saddle. "They are on the rocks where we always stand. Be careful. The rocks are wet."

Pulling his torch from the crevice where he had wedged it, Wallen went for the fish, brought them, and tied the bag across Twi's back. The two youths started down the trail home, Wallen leading the horse through the darkness.

"You did not fall in by accident, did you?" Wallen asked at last. "I saw Sigbert come back just at sunset."

"He pushed me in," Luthwin said.

"He has been saying trouble would come to you. I guess he had to make sure his prophecy came true."

"But how did you know I had gone fishing?"

Wallen swung the torch around to look at him. "God sent me. You said that yourself. When I saw you leave this morning, I was disappointed because I could not go with you. All day I thought you must be in danger. When Sigbert came back looking so pleased, I knew what he had done. It was as if God told me I must come to find you."

"Then you believe?" Luthwin knew his voice trembled with excitement.

"I guess I have always believed, even before the bishop came. But I did not want to think about anything so serious as religion. I wanted to think only about exciting, happy things."

"This is the happiest thing in the world to think about," Luthwin said. "The way of Christ is a happy way. It is a way of light and life more rich than any other way. It takes fear out of life."

"I began to see that when I interpreted for Brother Aiden. Luthwin, I wish I could translate all my life for the good teacher."

Luthwin did not tell Hunwold until the next day what Sigbert had done. "He will no longer live!" Hunwold exploded, his eyes smoldering. He pulled his sword from his sheath and rubbed its blade between his fingers.

"The law of heaven says, 'Do not kill,' " Luthwin reminded him.

"But he has sat at my table, enriched by my gifts and my goods for thirty years. He has gone with my men to battle," Hunwold exclaimed. "I must have vengeance!"

His son shook his head. He understood how his father felt, how the old way of life took hold of his feelings. "But this is not the Christian way," he explained. He stood before his father. Hesitantly he took the sword from Hunwold's hand. "We must just be careful of Sigbert. When he knows that I have come back to witness against him, he will be desperate."

"You must stay in your mother's quarters until I have spoken to Sigbert." Hunwold took him to the bower. "I will speak with you later, my son."

Luthwin waited with his mother. "You are catching a cold," she said, noticing his sniffling. "Did you get wet while you fished last night? You were late coming home."

"I got into the water," Luthwin remarked, silent until he remembered the parchment. Asking for his mother to get it for him from the oak chest, he unrolled it and looked at the words.

"I have just heard today," his mother said, "that Brother Aiden has land for a school. King Oswald gave him the island of Lindisfarne for his mission, and already they have begun building shelters for the young men who will come there to study. Brother Aiden has received twelve helpers from Iona to help him with the school. As soon as he is ready, you must go, Luthwin."

"Do you suppose Hunwold will let me go yet this year?"

His mother smiled. "Early this morning he commanded a ceorl to take materials for a small building where you may live, and he has made preparations to send food supplies for the school. Brother Aiden will expect you."

Luthwin's heart jumped. This time going to school would be different. He would not be confused as he had been at Edwin's royal villa when Deacon James tried to teach him. Nor would he be yearning to go home the way he did at Iona. No fear would keep his mind from his lessons. And now he had a reason to learn. He must get ready for a special purpose. He would learn to read well enough to understand the Scriptures and tell what he found in them to all his family. If only Wallen could go with him! He knew his friend would learn faster than he could, for Wallen could understand the teachers' language easily.

Midafternoon Hunwold called for Luthwin. "Come, speak before Sigbert, my son," he said. "He has said you are mistaken. He says he did not threaten or push you into the river."

Luthwin thought before he spoke. "Then why did he rush away to leave me to drown in the rapids?" He looked at Sigbert, but the priest turned his eyes away.

"I feared you were drowned already and beyond my help."

"And why did you not tell my father of what you saw?"

Hunwold's eyes bored into the priest's face. "You spoke not a word to me," he accused. "And at first you denied seeing Luthwin at all."

"I feared you would blame me."

Luthwin's father glared. "When have I been unjust with the men who have served me?" he thundered. "When have I dealt harshly with those who sat at my own table? When have I punished before seeking counsel of the whole assembly and finding all the truth?"

A thane paused at the door, embarrassed, Luthwin noticed, to see that he had interrupted a heated argument. But his business seemed urgent, for he called to Hunwold.

"Come in, Elfric," Hunwold said.

The thane looked at Sigbert standing uneasily before the eorl, his face red, his hands shaking. "Come, my lord," Elfric said, "when it is convenient for you to see what some enemy has done in the new church. Just now Wilfrig and Dedher came upon a heap of tinder while they inspected yesterday's work."

Sigbert made a quick movement as if he thought he could escape.

"Halt!" Hunwold grabbed a spear from beside his seat. "If you would have mercy from us, do not run, for it will prove you guilty." He waved for Luthwin to come with him and marched Sigbert out of the hall ahead of him to the chapel.

"Here!" Dedher said, pointing to a pile of flax and straw soaked with oil. "Someone planned to use this for tinder. He must have been called unexpectedly before he could set it afire."

Hunwold gripped Sigbert's arm. "The council will judge."

When Luthwin rose the next morning, Sigbert had gone with all his belongings, banished to the land of the Scots forever, Hunwold said. "For from now on, if he enters Bernicia, he will be an outlaw whom anyone may justly kill."

"He will find no eager listeners among the Scots," Luthwin commented. "Nearly all the Dalradians have become Christians now."

"Yes," his father said. "That is the best place we could send him. From there he will not raise a band of enemies to raid our borders. Has your mother told you, Luthwin, of our plans for you?"

"That I am going to school at Lindisfarne?"

Hunwold smiled. "I see you are glad with our decision."

"I could wish for only one other thing." Luthwin paused. He knew he did not need to explain to his father. His father knew his heart well enough to guess.

"Brother Aiden has already spoken for you, my son. When I asked what I might send to him as a gift, he said he needed Wallen to interpret his words to our people. I have promised him that if Wallen is willing to go, he shall be freed from his slavery for the sake of the work of God."

Luthwin felt like shouting. "Thank you, Father." He could say nothing more for a moment. All the words caught on the lump in his throat.

"I have not yet told Wallen. Would you like to ask him yourself?"

Luthwin nodded. He must not cry. But happiness welled up inside him until he had no more room for all the joy he felt.

"God, my Maker," he prayed as he left the hall, "thank You for this best gift You have given."

The weeks passed. A messenger brought word that Lindisfarne was ready for the young men who wished to study there. The school would welcome the sons of all men—sons of ceorls or thanes as well as the sons of eorls and princes. It would accept even slaves, for in Christ all were equal.

Hunwold sent Luthwin and Wallen, together with all those from the ton who wished to go. In a large cart they piled enough supplies to last through the coming winter. And old Thundor led the three teams of oxen. He, too, was a gift for the school.

Soon Luthwin felt at home in his new stone hut, which he shared with Wallen. The progress he made surprised him. Within a short time he could read simple words with ease. And he learned to understand the strange sounds of Latin so that he could read the Scriptures for himself. Surely God was helping him.

* * * * *

Luthwin held the ancient sword to the light. Brother Aiden looked at the letters on the blade.

"Yes, these are indeed Latin words," he said. He tilted the blade a little to see even better. "For the cause of Christ," he read.

He looked at Luthwin and then at Wallen. "You say this sword belonged to Hunwold's grandfather when he came with the invaders from across the channel? That is strange. The Saxons knew nothing of Christ then. And the letters look like those of a Roman smith of long ago. If you had not told me, I would have guessed the sword belonged to Wallen's grandfather. It is very old, for we no longer shape our letters just this way."

The teacher's face showed his puzzlement. Luthwin looked at Wallen and smiled. "Maybe you had a right to it all along."

"Do you suppose he took it from a Briton?" Wallen asked.

Aiden was thoughtful for a moment. "He could have."

Luthwin suddenly laughed. "What would Sigbert think if he knew he had tried to put a runic curse beside these words?" He held the sword so that he could read: "For the cause of Christ."

"Those words," said Aiden, "are stronger than any curse or magic. They are even stronger than any blade of steel a man can forge. The Scriptures speak of a sword." He laid his hand on Wallen's shoulder. "And, lad, you will be carrying that sword, the Word of God."

He placed his other hand on Luthwin. "And you shall be a great student of the Word. Someday you will teach other youths this Word with great zeal."

Luthwin felt a warmth of happiness filling his heart. The brother's face glowed with his prophecy. "This is better than to be a warrior," Luthwin said. "God has chosen us to work for Him."

Aiden shook his head. "You will yet be warriors, lads. You will yet carry a sword and conquer. God's blessings rest on your warfare. You will gain victories in His name!"